Your Cheatin Hearts
by
Linn Random

Published by Sanibel Press www.SanibelPress.com
318 E Orange Street, Altamonte Springs, Fl 32701

Second e-published by Sanibel Press January 2007
First Print Publishing January 2007

www.SanibelPress.com

This is a work of fiction. Names, characters, places, and incidents are the
product of the author's imagination. Any resemblance to persons living
or dead, business establishments, events, or locals is entirely coincidental.
All characters in this book have no existence outside the imagination of
the author and have no relation whatsoever to anyone bearing the same
name or names.

Printed in the U.S.A.

LINN RANDOM

YOUR CHEATIN HEARTS

www.SanibelPress.com

2007

Your Cheatin Hearts

Ecataromance Reviewers Choice Award for 2005, Cupids, 5 Stars, 5 Unicorns

"Maggie Colter," Sarah her voice was stern in warning. "We've been best friends since we were in pigtails. I've been with you on every crazy adventure you've had, but this one takes the cake!"

"Everyone has grandchildren," Maggie said pointedly, "everyone! The women at the Guild, Sunday school, all our friends, YOU!"

"Jack just hasn't met the right girl yet," Sarah offered, trying to keep pity out of her voice.

"The right girl! The right girl! That boy of mine is 31 years old! And I am tired of waiting! It's high time I take matters into my own hands. Whether you think this is a fool plan or not I'm going to see this through!"

With a glint in her blue eyes, Maggie raised her chin. "I don't care. I have waited for him long enough to make up his mind. Now it's up to me."

Sarah shook her head. "Well do you have anyone in mind?"

Maggie brightened prettily. "As a matter of fact I do. I saw my attorney, you know Emmett Smith, don't you? Well just the other day I saw him talking to a pretty girl at the courthouse. Just Jack's type."

"Outside the courthouse? Heavens to Betsy, Maggie! She could be a murderer or a criminal for all you know."

"I'm not going to listen to another word from you Sarah; I thought you of all people would be helpful." Maggie sniffed as she took a sip of her coffee, "besides, but I know my son, and Jack will find her attractive. She's smart and she has her own business. My future daughter-in-law is a private investigator!"

"That poor boy," Sarah said, shaking her head. "I remember how hurt he was when he found out his college sweetheart was cheating with another fella. Maggie, I wonder if Jack is ever going to trust a girl again no matter how pretty she is."

"Good grief, Sarah, that was years ago. Now I am going to find out more about her, then I have to come up with a way to get her and Jack together. This time next year, I will be holding my first grandchild. Wait and see!"

ACKNOWLEDGEMENTS
To Readers:

For years it was my privilege and great joy to live in Hendersonville, North Carolina. Some of my happiest memories, those dearest to my heart are with friends I made in this beautiful mountain town.

The Pisgah Inn

Many, many a weekend was spent happily on The Blue Ridge Parkway where my son and I would always stop at the Pisgah Inn. High atop Mount Pisgah, it offers visitors one of the most beautiful views of the Blue Ridge Mountains. The restaurant is as I have described in my book and you will discover the food is delicious and the staff and management are friendly. If you are diving on The Blue Ridge Parkway, do stop to enjoy the scenery, purchase a real mountain craft or souvenir from the gift shop or enjoy a lovely meal at the Pisgah Inn. I want to personally thank Bruce O'Connell for allowing me to use The Pisgah Inn in my book, Your Cheatin Hearts. For more information about the history, to make reservations or information please visit the Pisgah Inn at www.pisgahinn. com. The Pisgah Inn is truly one of my favorite places.

The Grove Park Inn Resort & Spa

I also want to acknowledge The Grove Park Inn Resort & Spa in Asheville. I enjoyed visited this beautiful resort many times for luncheons, dinners and conferences. It's timeless in its beauty and truly one of the most glamorous and beautiful resorts in the world.

I wish to thank the staff, management for their superb service, wonderful memories and for the privilege of allowing me to feature The Grove Park Inn Resort & Spa in my novel, Your Cheatin' Hearts. Special thanks to Marketing Communications Assistant, Shelby Thompson who helped me in making my scene accurate.

For more information on The Grove Park Inn Resort & Spa and the beautiful Sunset Terrace, please visit www. groveparkinn.com

Hendersonville, North Carolina

Though I live in Florida now, part of my heart will always be in this beautiful mountain town. For More Information about Hendersonville, North Carolina, visit www. historichendersonville.org

PROLOGUE

Maggie Colter," Sarah Donavan cried. "Have you lost your mind?"

With her outburst a warm cup of coffee that Sarah Donavan had been holding crashed onto the table of Carter's Drug Emporium. The creamy Colombian blend flooded the counter top, spilling over its edge. Those clustered in small pairs at the counter bar gasped and children giggled.

At the table, Sarah and her companion began pulling the almost invisible sheaths of white napkins out of the dispenser in an ill-fated attempt to stop the flow from reaching their purses, their laps, and the floor of the luncheonette.

From behind the counter, like a Valkyrie, brandishing a dull dish towel in her hand, Rachel Cunningham, Carter's only waitress and quick order cook ran toward the table. Breathless with rage, her brown eyes had taken on a demonic glow and were wide with fury. Her pinched nose was flaring with fury. And a few would later say they saw small puffs of smoke emerging from her ears.

"Here, let me!" her voice rang throughout the drugstore like an echo from an empty tomb. Glaring down at both women, she deftly began cleaning up the spill taking great care not to spoil her starched white uniform.

With the claustrophobe averted, she clinched hands and rested them squarely on her broad hips. She glared at Sarah, "I suppose you would like another cup?"

The collective gasp from everyone seated at the counter broke the still silence in the small café. They held their breath, waiting for Sarah's reply.

Sarah looked down at her empty cup. She truly did want a cup of coffee but hesitated a moment before asking for it.

"Well," Sarah began, "if you don't mind."

The men at the countertop grinned and the women looked away ready to shield their children's eyes from what would come next.

Rachel stood towering above the red Formica table. Carter's was post-war chic. Post Vietnam War. To the passing tourist, Carter's Drug Store was retro. They would never have guessed the luncheonette was still using the same equipment that had been installed during the 1950s.

The popular downtown drug store was an institution, as was Rachel Cunningham. Those who patronized Carter's knew also not to trouble Rachel for added service. She stood towering over Sarah Cunningham.

For a paused moment the two women stared one another in a Mexican standoff, then with a sudden and sharp turn with wet range in hand, Rachel picked up the white porcelain cup and walked leisurely toward the counter.

Sarah watched her go knowing full well the story of the spill would be repeated oft times in the next several days to anyone who would listen. She didn't care. She wanted that cup of coffee whether it annoyed Rachel or not.

"I don't know why that woman has a job here," Sarah said with a sigh. "She hates waiting on people. Why doesn't the old bat just retire like the rest of us?"

Sarah turned back to her friend of almost fifty years and frowned. Remembering why she had spilled the stupid cup in the first place she leaned across the table and in a hiss, whispered, "Now, Maggie Colter, tell me you are not serious."

Maggie Colter smiled. Time had been good to Maggie Colter. With soft gray hair that curled in ringlets and the lines that graced her face were easily covered with makeup. Acknowledging her slight spread, she preferred to say she was fluffy instead of plump. Once one of the town's premier belles, she had aged graciously, though the mischief that once sparkled brightly in her five year old eyes now glittered like exquisite diamonds as she approached sixty.

"Maggie," Sarah repeated, this time her voice barring no quarter. "Tell me you aren't seriously going to do this."

"Yes, I am. And don't you dare look at me all pomp and smug. I'm the only woman left in Western North Carolina without grandchildren!" Maggie wailed. She knew any faint-hearted plea for sympathy would not fool her long time friend.

Rachel Cunningham returned to the table saving Maggie from further comment.

"Your coffee," Rachel Cunningham said, unceremoniously placing a fresh cup on the table. Rachel scowled at Sarah one last time as though daring her to spill the new cup.

Sarah offered Rachel a weak smile. Rachel raised her eyebrow and with a look of pure contempt turned and walked away.

"Maggie Colter," Sarah said, directing her attention back to her friend, "we've been best friends since we were in pigtails. I've been with you on every crazy adventure you've had but this one takes the cake! You can't be serious!"

"Oh hush up!" Maggie said, seething with renewed resolve. "Everyone I know has grandchildren. And I want at least one!"

"What about that nice Jenny Fields that Jack had been seeing last year?" Sarah asked. "What happened with her?"

"Nothing, Jenny was just a friend and she is engaged to some boy from Marshall. Jack was just coaching her son's baseball team. I thought when he told me he was going to coach a soccer team; I was hoping he'd have scored one of those divorced soccer moms. Who would have guessed he had the only team in town with married women?"

Sarah looked sympathetically at her friend.

"Everyone has grandchildren," Maggie said pointedly, "everyone! The women at the Guild, Sunday school, all our friends, YOU!"

"Well," Sarah offered as though trying to keep pity out of her voice. "Jack just hasn't met the right girl."

"The right girl? The right girl! He's almost 31 years old! And I am tired to waiting! It's high time I take matters into my own hands. Whether you think this is a fool errand or not, I'm going to see this through!"

"Maggie, really, I wish you'd rethink this. You can lead that good-looking boy of yours to water, but he might not drink and he sure as heck isn't going to like you interfering in his love life. You know how stubborn he is. This time you'll really get him riled up Maggie. He might not speak to you for years. Have you thought about that?"

With a glint in her eyes, Maggie raised her chin. "I don't care. I've waited for him long enough. Now it's up to me."

Sarah shook her head. "Well do you have anyone in mind?"

Maggie brightened prettily. "As a matter of fact I do. I saw my attorney, you know Emmett Smith, don't you? A little over a week ago, I saw him talking to a pretty girl at the courthouse. Just Jack's type, and I found out she's single."

Sarah stared at Maggie. "Outside the courthouse? Oh my goodness, Maggie, this woman could be an ax murderer. A real criminal for all you know."

"No, she's not a murderer. In fact she has her own business! My future daughter-in-law is a private investigator. Imagine that? Now finish your coffee before it gets cold."

"Oh dear," Sarah said, shaking her head. "I remember how hurt he was when he found out his college sweetheart was cheating with another fella. Maggie, I wonder if Jack is ever going to trust a girl again no matter how pretty she is."

"Good grief, Sarah, that was years ago. Now I'm going to find out more about her. Then I have to come up with plan to get her and Jack together. Once I get them together, I'll let nature take its course. And Miss Sarah," Maggie smugly assured her friend, "whether he likes it or not, this time next year, Jack Colter will be married! And, he will be happy! I'll have my grandchildren! Sarah, you and all you grandmothers of this town just watch me. This time next year, I will be holding my first grandchild. Wait and see!"

CHAPTER ONE

Mrs. Colter," Shelby MacGregor said, trying not to sound impatient, "on the phone you said this was a matter of life and death."

"Oh? Did I say that?" Maggie Colter stammered almost as if taken by surprise. The older woman leaned back against her the seat at the Wayside Restaurant. She seemed a bit confused and quiet as though she were contemplating her reply.

Shelby remained silent. Meeting a private investigator for the first time made a lot of people nervous. In three years of heading her own agency, *Your Cheatin Hearts*, she knew she could learn a lot by nervous chatter and gain valuable insight into perspectives' personalities. This was also crucial, for if she discovered their spouse was cheating, it was imperative she know how her clients would react to the unhappy news.

Maggie Colter was different; she had no spouse. She did, however, need her help. Her call came just this morning. It was a matter of life or death she had pleaded. Now Maggie Colter sat hesitant and unresponsive. Moments passed. Maggie Colter twisted the amethyst ring on her finger then licked her lips. Her distress was unmistakable.

Shelby sat patiently watching her.

Despite her casual attire, the woman before her was probably one of the well-to-do women in this small Western North Carolina mountain town. In her late fifties, Maggie Colter's face was just beginning to wrinkle. Her blue eyes were soft but troubled.

Maggie took a sip of coffee and scanned the dining room before nervously placed the coffee cup back in its saucer.

Shelby waited a moment more. Meeting a private investigator even without the trench coat, smoking cigarettes, or in a back alley unnerved the best of people.

Shelby took note of Maggie's plump hands. Though manicured, they looked used. Shelby suspected Maggie loved to garden. This was a woman who no doubt enjoyed living life on her own terms. Sensing a kindred spirit, Shelby looked back to Maggie and shifted slightly against the booth. This was Maggie's cue to talk but she didn't take it.

Shelby wondered what had prompted this woman to make her frantic call. She was hiding something. What or more importantly, why?

She cleared her throat. "Mrs. Colter, is your son's life in jeopardy?"

Suddenly Maggie Colter's eyes widened, her round face lit with delight. "Yes! That's it! My son is in definite danger, Ms. MacGregor."

The image of Jack Colter flashed in Shelby's mind. She had seen him around town. Though she had never been formally introduced, she concluded the ruggedly handsome Jack Colter hardly appeared a man that needed protecting.

"Your son is in danger?" Shelby asked, and heard the doubt in her voice. She suddenly had the nagging suspicion that Maggie Colter was making her story up as she went along.

The waitress returned with their order. She placed a large slice of the praline pecan pie in front of Maggie.

"Sure you don't want something, honey?" the waitress drawled in a soft southern accent to Shelby. Shelby shook her head. With a slight tilt of her head, the waitress laid the check on the table and hurried toward a couple who had just walked in the door.

"Are you sure you don't want anything besides that Diet Coke, dear?" Maggie asked, lifting up her fork.

Shelby shook her head. Maggie turned her attention back to the praline pie. With the dexterity and grace of a matador, Maggie removed her napkin from the table and laid it across her lap. Whatever was troubling Maggie Colter seemed momentarily forgotten as she slid the fork into the thick, dark pie.

"Mrs. Colter," Shelby persisted. "If your son is in danger, you should be talking to the police."

"Oh no! I can't!" She protested too quickly. "Jack would be furious. By the way, my friends call me Maggie, please do as well. And, may I call you Shelby?"

Without giving her a chance to respond, Maggie immediately turned her attention back to her first bite of the pie.

"Hum," Maggie cooed, "this is so good. You know, The Wayside always has the best pie. Did I mention my son is not married?"

"Mrs. Colter," Shelby began in a huskier and she hoped more serious tone. "Maggie, you said your son is in danger?"

"Tell me more about yourself, my dear," Maggie mumbled between bites. "Being a private investigator and all must be a very dangerous profession. Does your boyfriend mind?"

Shelby shook her head no. "There's no boyfriend, fiancé, or husband in my life. No child. Nothing that would distract me from your son's welfare."

Maggie stopped eating her pie. She took her fork and with great care laid it across her plate. Her jaw tensed and her eyebrows arched as she asked, "But you do like children, don't you?"

"Yes, I like children very much, Mrs. Colter," Shelby assured her, noticing the visible look of relief on the older woman's face. "Maggie, if you believe your son's life is in danger, you need to be having this conversation with the police. Not with me. My firm, *Your Cheatin Hearts* specializes in infidelity."

"Hum, yes well, your brochure said you were with law enforcement for a while."

"I was," Shelby explained in a voice that was cool and calm, "four years to be exact, but I didn't go into criminology to specialized training to write parking tickets. I moved into private investigation work. I work for some of Western North Carolina's most prestigious employers, doing background checks and advising them on plant security. However, my primary business is devoted to husbands and wives who suspect their partners are cheating. Hence, the name, *Your Cheatin Hearts*."

Maggie looked surprised. "Is there a lot of that going on?"

Shelby couldn't help but smile. Maggie's innocence was genuine. "Unfortunately, yes."

"Oh my," Maggie stammered. She looked for a moment as if she were ready to order another slice of pie.

"Maggie, perhaps you would like to see my credentials," Shelby said, changing the subject. "You can rely on my discretion. And, again, if your son's life is in danger then I would strongly suggest you talk to the police."

"No, dear, they won't help at all," Maggie replied, her eyes filled with certainty. Several pensive moments passed before Maggie offered Shelby a radiant smile. "Emmett Smith, my attorney, recommended you. Now that I've seen you, I think you are just perfect for what I need."

Shelby made a mental note to send Emmett a thank you card for his referral. She remained quiet.

For a moment, Maggie was deep in thought as if contemplating her next reply. Shelby suspected she was stalling. After taking another bite, Maggie reached in her oversized purse and pulled out an envelope.

"Here," she said, passing an oversized brown envelope to Shelby. "This might help. Just look at this and tell me what you think."

Shelby accepted the package and let its contents slide across the table. A full four color photo of the 6'1" Jack Colter spilled out of the envelope. Shelby picked up the picture noting how handsome Jack Colter was.

"The advertising agency that helps us with the catalog likes to use Jack for photos," Maggie stated with maternal pride.

Shelby studied the pictures of one of Hendersonville's most eligible and successful bachelors. In spite of his other attributes, Jack Colter was certainly photogenic.

In the photo layout, Jack managed a relaxed poise for the camera with one long leg rigid on the ground and the other resting on the log. His smile was captivating and his arresting good looks fully captured her attention. The Blue Ridge Mountains served as a dramatic backdrop.

He wore a tan shirt with matching pants that fit him snug about his narrow waist and hips. The hiking boots were new but anyone looking scene could see he was a man well suited for the wilderness.

Leaning against his muscular thigh, his arms even in this casual pose looked hard and powerful. From his wide shoulders to broad chest, to his firm abs, he seemed unaware of his male virility.

Shelby thought with his natural good looks and rugged physique, he could have had a successful career as a male model.

She found it hard to avoid the steady warm gaze of his electric blue eyes. He was tanned, no, Shelby corrected herself, bronzed. Devoid of tan lines, he had the appearance of someone who worked outdoors without a shirt. His lips were not full, but appeared soft, and easily kissable. She blushed, embarrassed to find Maggie smiling at her.

Looking very pleased, Maggie's eyes were sparkling with sheer delight. "I told you he was nice looking, didn't I?"

Shelby drew an uneasy breath. Drawn back the photo, Jack seemed to be teasing her now. The blue fire in his eyes warmed his smile and somehow made the neatly square jaw softer. His neck was strong, and like the rest of his body, muscular and athletic.

Jack Colter's soft dark hair was cropped and short around his ears and face. It was a style that demanded little keep and suited him well.

His hands looked enormous and strong. Without meaning to, Shelby wondered what it would be like to be touched by those fingers and gathered into those muscular arms. With one more appreciative glance at the photo, she laid the picture aside. She was confident Jack Colter was a man who could take care of himself.

Seeing Maggie beaming at her, she knew she had showed entirely too much interest in the handsome Jack Colter. "Did I mention Jack is not married? Of course, I did; well, no matter. And Shelby, you know honey, I couldn't help but notice that picture in your brochure. You are so much prettier in person. Has anyone ever told you that you look a bit like Jaclyn Smith? Much prettier though, I think. Your features are softer, nicer."

Shelby gave her a half smile. They were not here to discuss her but her son. Quick to return the topic to Jack, Shelby asked, "Maggie, do you suspect your son is being followed?"

Maggie bolted upright. A look of pure delight sparkled in her brown eyes. "Yes, that's it! My son is being followed! Why didn't I think...well, what I meant to tell you earlier. Yes, I'm definitely going to need you to watch my son for several days. A week! Maybe a month or so, maybe longer, however long it takes!"

Shelby sat unmoved. Had this just occurred to her? She was not at all convinced Jack was in serious danger. Again, she sensed that Maggie was hiding something from her.

"All right, then, if you are serious, my fee is $ 275 a day," Shelby said, hoping the amount would discourage any tomfoolery.

Maggie didn't blink.

Shelby continued, "My schedule is free at the moment. We should know in a matter of days whether your son is being followed or not."

"Oh no, dear, I'm quite sure I'll need more time than that," Maggie protested as she reached in her pocketbook and pulled her checkbook out.

Shelby sat puzzled; perhaps the handsome Jack Colter was in danger after all.

"Okay, Maggie," she said evenly, "if I do find out someone is following your son, we may need to go the police. Agreed?"

"Oh yes," Maggie stammered too quickly, "absolutely! I agree."

Shelby took a long breath. "First, tell me, why do you believe someone is following your son? Is he aware of this? If he's not, then we need to discuss this with him right away."

Maggie shook her head. Her brows drew together in an agonized expression. "No, no, no, no, he mustn't know. If he finds out I've been meddling again he'll be very angry at me."

Maggie leaned across the table and said in a low whisper, "We need to keep this between us."

Shelby frowned. "Do you have any idea why someone would be following your son? Is Jack into gambling, drugs, any type of criminal or illegal dealings? Anything I should know about?"

"Heavens, no," Maggie replied in a voice that was clear and exact, "Jack has never been involved in anything like that. I suppose you have to ask those sorts of questions? No, no, my Jack's a good boy. Now if you look in the envelope, I brought you information about his schedule. I thought that would be helpful."

Maggie glanced at her watch, handed Shelby the check. She then placed a five and several ones on the table to cover her pie, their drinks, and the tip.

"Here's my check, dear, that should cover you for a week or so. I just need you to follow my son and tell me what you think."

"Mrs. Colter," Shelby protested. "Maggie, you have given me too much for a few days work. If I conclude earlier than you are anticipating, I'll return any unused part of the retainer to you. As to whether your son is being followed, we'll know in a matter of days."

Impulsively Maggie leaned over and gave Shelby a tight hug.

"My dearest Shelby, I know all this seems confusing and a bit of a surprise for you, but I will assure you, at the end of the day, it will all be well. You'll see."

With her last comment, she pulled away from Shelby, gave her a broad smile, turned, and walked away.

Watching Maggie leave the restaurant, Shelby sat unable to shake the feeling that there was more to Maggie's story than she had offered. With two years of law enforcement and three years in her own private detective agency, Shelby knew the woman was hiding something. What, she wondered, but more importantly, why? Whatever Maggie was keeping from her, she would know in a matter of days. One thing she had learned in life was the truth always comes out. Always.

Watching Maggie Colter walk away she felt uneasy. In her line of work, a lot of people claimed to want to know the truth then denied it even when faced with documented facts and photos. There were a dozen reasons why any human being wanted to watch another. In the next several days, Shelby would know why Maggie wanted her son followed. And if someone was indeed following Jack Colter, she would not only find out who; but more importantly, why.

About to leave the table, she caught a faint glimpse of her reflection in the restaurant's window. Her sable brown hair curled in layers about her face and hung just below shoulders. She swept it over her collar thinking if she had the time later she would get it cut. The soft show of violet that had once graced her eyes as a child had gone, replaced by a look that to her seemed harder. She didn't care...or did she?

Jaclyn Smith, she smiled remembering Maggie's comparison, indeed! She watched as her soft full lips curled into a smile.

At least through it all she had been true to herself and her promise. She would never love again.

It had been years since she thought of Jared. Jared, with his movie star good looks and his easy smile had won a younger Shelby. How innocent she must have seemed to him. How utterly vulnerable.

Well no more, she thought with a smile, no more and never, never again!

Built on her broken heart, she now kept other women from being the fool she had been by catching cheaters in her small town of Hendersonville. Business was flourishing.

Unlike her glamorous TV counterparts, Shelby didn't drive a fancy sports car, or have an enormous staff to assist her. Like most P.I.s in America, she ran a small one man, correction, one woman shop. She had done quite well for herself in the beautiful mountains of Western North Carolina. In fact, she thought proudly, she had moved out of her house a year and a half ago to open a small storefront office close to the courthouse. While the storefront was mostly for show, it was close to several attorneys she worked for. It was these same attorneys who recommended her services to clients either prior to, during, or after a divorce. Whether it was for "cheating," hiding assets from a spouse, or investigating a new person in their children's life, there was always ample need for her services. Shelby liked her little storefront office; it gave her respectability in a sometimes disreputable business.

Clients, especially new ones, preferred not to be seen walking in and out of her office. More often than not, she met potential clients at the various restaurants around town. Maggie Colter, who had called her just this morning, was one of them.

Though she had never formally met Maggie Colter, she was familiar with her and her son, Jack. They were the owners of Bear Creek Outfitters. Their one time general store had grown from a small town mercantile to a now successful store and national catalog sales, offering its customers everything from state of the art camping equipment to flannel shirts, jeans, and fashionable outdoor wear.

Both Maggie and her son, Jack, were known as generous benefactors to the town, especially with children's groups and church organizations.

Shelby finished her Diet Coke and pocketed the check into her purse.

Less than five minutes later, she was in her Chevy Tracker headed toward town. On the drive, she began to plot how and when to start monitoring Jack Colter's movements.

With the packet of information beside her, she drove back toward her office and called Chris Thompson at the Hendersonville Police Department.

The dispatcher patched her through to her part-time employee and former partner. Chris Thompson moonlighted with her on cases that required 24 hour surveillance.

"Shelby!" Chris answered when he answered her call. "How are you doing?"

"Great, can you give me some time over the next three days? Mostly evening work."

"You bet! Who and where?"

"I'll call you later. And, you will be surprised as to who."

"I doubt that, Shelby." Chris said with a laugh. "I'll plan on being available for you this evening."

Ending the call, she pulled onto Main Street, barely noticing the charming ambiance of small town Americana. It was Wednesday afternoon and unlike her big city counterparts, most Hendersonville stores closed midday as was the custom. Still, she saw a few shoppers going door to door.

Bear Creek Outfitters was open and business was brisk with tourists and a few locals.

Slowly driving past the entrance, she noted the vehicles parked in front, but nothing seemed out of place. Taking the full drive down Main Street, she turned left at Second, and circled the entire downtown area. This time, she passed Main Street, and drove down Church Street to a huge parking lot behind Bear Creek Outfitters.

Grabbing a bottle of water from her cooler, Shelby pulled out the packet of information on Jack Colter and gave his photo an appreciative glance.

No daydreaming allowed, she told herself. With a wistful sigh, she put the photo to the back of the packet.

She read the itinerary but it gave no clue as to why Jack would be followed. It appeared he worked all the time and seemed to have little if any social life.

Around 6:00 p.m., she noticed Jack Colter emerge from the store. The photo was a poor copy of the man. In real life, his shoulders were broader, his hips slimmer, and he looked far more muscular than the picture had offered. Shelby, who had sworn off men, couldn't help but admire the way he moved in his tight- fitting jeans. At least the strikingly handsome Jack Colter was a refreshing change from the portly men she was usually assigned to watch. Do your job, she reminded herself; Jack Colter is not for you.

He looked back at the store and waved goodbye at the older man before he pulled his white Ford Bronco out of the parking lot.

Shelby started the Tracker and pulled out behind him, careful to leave two to three cars between them to avoid suspicion. No one seemed to be following him. When he reached home, he pulled into the driveway, parked his SUV, and went into the house. She watched as lights went on, following his movements through the house. Nothing seemed out of the ordinary.

It had been a long day for Jack Colter and surprisingly, one that left him pensive and reflective of his life, or as he mused, the lack of one.

There was the Father and Son Fishing Tournament the coming weekend and it seemed every father and son in town had made it a point to come in to buy their son a first fishing pole from Bear Creek Outfitters.

The activity of men sizing up the poles, showing their boys how to cast, and purchasing their sons' first tackle boxes had gotten to him by the end of the day.

Watching the scene replay a half dozen times throughout the afternoon reminded him all the more that he didn't have a son, a family other than his mother, and he didn't even have a woman in his life.

Unexpectedly he thought back to Celeste, his long time high school and college sweetheart. He had been just about ready to pop the question when he learned his all too perfect, all too beautiful Celeste had been two timing him with another man. He had been devastated. His boyish infatuation with Celeste was long gone. In its place was the only residual of a deep distrust of women. Shortly after discovering her infidelity, he vowed to never love again, but surprising even himself, the thought of a woman to come home to, a child to love, was growing more appealing with each year.

As he opened the Bronco's door, his mouth thinned with displeasure, he had given Celeste enough of his life. Maybe it was time to begin a new one. His mother had been on his case for several years now to find someone and start a family, and the Father and Son Fishing Tournament certainly reminded him of what he was missing.

Humm, he thought with a long intake of breath as he pulled out into traffic, his house was big enough, he would liked to see it filled with children, a son or sons to take to a fishing tournament, and it would be nice to have someone waiting at home instead of returning to an empty, dark house every night.

On the drive home, he tried to concentrate on the traffic, but his thoughts kept drifting back to his own isolation and options about changing it. He knew he wasn't going to find the future mother of his children in a bar. He went at odd hours to the health club and in his circle of acquaintances could think of no one who could fit the role. Maybe he would attend the next Chamber of Commerce Meeting next month or even date one of the women his mother had suggested. After all, the girl of his dreams wouldn't just fall in front of him, would she?

Shelby looked at Jack Colter's home. It was one of the grand old stately homes built by South Carolinians who came to Hendersonville at the turn of the century to escape the heat of the low country.

Beautiful green ferns graced the wrap around porch. The large white house gave the appearance of being recently painted. Only the blue shutters and gray rooftop accented the home. The yard, except for a few azaleas, was manicured but hardly landscaped as the almost identical home next door. Both were two stories. Many of these magnificent homes had been converted to quaint bed and breakfasts.

Beautiful homes, Shelby thought as she parked her Tracker at an empty lot across the street. She grabbed a Rae Monet novel she had been reading and settled back for what she hoped would be a quiet night.

As the hours passed, she made note of the vehicles which moved about the neighborhood.

She called Chris Thompson close to the end of his shift and gave him the address where she needed him that night.

"You've got to be kidding," he said when he pulled up behind her around 10 p.m. "Jack Colter's a boy scout. Who wants you to keep tabs on him?"

"His mother. She suspects someone is following him. Just keep your eyes open, okay?"

"Will do," Chris said with a sigh.

Chris arrived about an hour later and Shelby waved her goodbye as she went to her home. "See you in the morning."

Chris nodded and settled back in his seat. Shelby knew he was the one man she could depend on.

It was just after 6:00 a.m. when she returned to find Chris blurry eyed staring at the Colter house.

"Go home," she said with a laugh. "Get some sleep. By the way, anything happen last night?"

"Pretty quiet," Chris said with a yawn. "Lights went out by 11:00. I did notice an old ford truck about 2:00 a.m.. Seemed a bit out of place for this neighborhood, especially that time of night; it made a full two passes before it drove away. I wrote down the license plate and will run it later today."

"I appreciate that," Shelby said with a glance toward the house. "Now you run on home and get some shut eye."

After Chris left, Shelby glanced at her watch. Dressed in running gear she got out of her car and stretched. The store didn't open until 9:00 a.m. Jack, according to his mother, never left the house before 8:00.

The day was still quiet. Crickets chirped and birds sang softly as if not to break the still of the cool Carolina morning. Lawns and trees were thickly laid in the honeyed mist of a new dawn. The sweet fragrance of flowers surrounded her like a loving friend, warm, comforting, and always there.

Realizing this was the only time she would probably have all day for exercise, she wasted no time in stretching before she began her daily run.

Not daring to roam far, she decided to take a fast run to the end of the long street, and returned. On the second pass, she saw a light go on in Jack's house. He was right on schedule. It was nearly 7:30. She decided to take one more turn through the neighborhood.

Kids were beginning to emerge from the houses, moving slowly down to the end of the street toward a bus stop. One boy pulled a skateboard from his arm and dropped it to the ground before gliding past her to a neighbor's house on the other side of Jack's home.

Checking her watch, she finished the last stretch to the end of the street and decided to run back.

As she neared Jack's house she noticed his white Ford Bronco driving slowly down the drive. She cursed softly under her breath, and pulled the baseball cap lower to cover her face. She kept her pace steady, her head down. As soon as she reached her Tracker, she would be able to follow him easily.

The Bronco stopped at the end of the driveway. It pulled forward as Shelby ran along side a neighbor's hedge-lined sidewalk.

Too late, she heard the scraping sounds of a skateboard. The boy on the skateboard burst onto the sidewalk directly in front of her.

As she jumped to avoid him, her foot landed off center on the curb. She was helpless but to fall forward directly into the path of the Ford Bronco. Her small frame twisted just before her body slammed against the pavement. Her shoulders and head took the brunt of the fall. She heard the screech of the brakes.

No, no, no, Shelby cried inside as she heard the Bronco's door open. She couldn't have fallen right in front of Jack Colter! She slowly opened her eyes to see his handsome face just inches from her. She closed her eyes. No, this couldn't be happening!

"Is she dead?" the skateboarder asked, managing to sound blameless for his part in the accident.

"She's not dead," Jack said impatiently to the teen, then to Shelby, "Miss, are you alright?"

"Yes, just a bump on my head," was all she could manage as she tried to rise. A sharp pain ran up the back of her neck. She fell back against the pavement.

"Should I call an ambulance?" a woman's voice rang out. The woman sounded strangely familiar. In fact, it sounded like Maggie Colter.

"No, we can get her to the doctor's office quicker," Jack said to the woman. Speaking back to her, she felt the warmth of his breath upon her cheek. "You hit your head pretty hard. Nothing looks broken. Can you stand up?"

"I think so," Shelby said, struggling to rise. For a second time, she fell back. Not wanting to, she slowly opened her eyes and focused on the deepest pair of blue eyes she had ever seen. God, he is handsome she thought with a smile. Her vision blurred.

As she faded to black, she heard the skateboarder proclaim, "Yep. You killed her Mister. She's dead."

CHAPTER TWO

S helby heard the murmur of voices but couldn't discern what was being said. As the words became clearer, the voices became more recognizable. A woman's voice sounded familiar. It sounded like Maggie Colter.

Before she could speculate as to how or why Maggie would be there, she heard two male voices. The first voice was older, softer, and more reserved with almost a gentle quality. The second voice sounded stronger and younger. Though she didn't recognize it there was a velvet quality about the second voice. She heard a second female voice address one of the men as Doctor.

Shelby wondered how long she could lay there with her eyes shut.

Slowly she opened her eyes and looked around. She was lying on a paper sheathe atop a hard examination table. Across from her she saw jars of cotton balls, tongue depressors, glass jars filled with swabs. All shared a countertop with several stainless steel containers. The walls were ivory. A drab, nondescript, floral picture barely broke the sterile environment. She was in a doctor's office. And, to her great misfortune she was not dead.

Panning the room, she focused on four distinct figures. An older man dressed in a white lab coat, a young nurse, and Maggie Colter wearing a floral housecoat.

Jack Colter stood behind the trio, his muscular arms

crossed and his lips taunt with grave concern. His presence dominated the room. As Shelby's eyes met his, his soft lips curled into a sensual smile. The warmth of his eyes swept over her, touching her in places she did not know existed. His blue eyes looked sharper against the dark navy shirt he was wearing. Even leaning against the wall, his casual stance was powerful in tight fitting jeans.

Knowing her cover was blown, she groaned. I'll give Maggie her money back, she thought as she tried to rise.

"I'm Doctor Edwards," the man in the lab coat said. "You've taken quite a bump on the head, nothing serious. How are you feeling?"

Shelby reached her hand back to her head and wrenched as she touched the swelling.

The doctor looked down at the chart and then back to her. "I don't think there's anything to worry about but I'd like to take some x-rays before you leave."

"I'm Jack Colter," Jack introduced himself; "you fell in front of my car. I brought you to the doctor's office. My mother and I live just around the corner. It was faster to drive you here than wait for paramedics."

Shelby turned her attention to Maggie.

"This is my mother," Jack said, noticing her eyes focusing on Maggie.

"No introductions necessary, Jack," Maggie announced to the surprise of everyone present. "I know this young lady."

Shelby was relieved. With the truth out, she would be able to move forward with her investigation after all.

"We met several days ago," Maggie said cheerfully. The fire in her eyes was radiant with insanity. "My new friend is the famous romance novelist, Silver Lake."

"What?" Shelby stammered, but no one seemed to notice.

"Oh my gosh!" the nurse cried, "Silver Lake! I've read all your books! I just finished the last in the *Founding of the Caribbean Series* when Cassandra's true love, Jamie McPherson was killed by the Pirate Prince. And then, oh my goodness, she was kidnapped by the Arab Sheik and was taken to his palace! Oh! Can I have your autograph?"

"You ...don't...that is. . . I'm not," Shelby said, but Maggie interrupted before she could finish.

"Don't say another word, Silver," Maggie admonished. Maggie looked to Jack, the doctor, and nurse. "Silver and I met several days ago. She's researching her new book here and we've become fast friends. Isn't that exciting?"

Jack's grin broadened to a radiant smile. He took a deep breath, grateful she was going to be all right!

Without meaning to he found himself captivated by her distinctly feminine outline. Her long, brown hair was luxurious and was partially hidden beneath an Atlanta Braves baseball cap. Loose tendrils escaped the cap and caressed her delicately shaped cheekbones. Her eyes were the color of deep, cool, liquid pools of mountain lake and he found them magnetic. It was impossible not to return her disarming smile.

Her appeal had piqued his interest at the moment of their introduction and though he tried not to look, he couldn't help but notice the soft curves of her body. Her hips tapered into the sculptured thighs and calves of an athlete.

He shouldn't be assessing the beautiful woman on the examining room table, especially since he'd almost run over her.

He smiled at her. "A romance novelist, I'm impressed."

"No," Shelby struggled to be heard, "I'm..."

"Going to stay with me for the next few days," Maggie finished for her. "Not another word! I insist!"

"Do you have family here, Ms. Lake?" the doctor asked.

"No, no family here," Shelby answered. Her mind seemed to be on a delayed response time. "But I need..."

"Of course you can stay with my mother. She's talked about you for years and has got to be your number one fan. Or," Jack offered with a mischievous grin, "you could stay with me. I have a big house and you'd be welcome."

He is flirting with me, Shelby thought in a daze. I'm lying on my death bed and he's flirting with me! Unexpectedly she felt her cheeks flush with warmth.

"Silver Lake, oh my gosh, Silver Lake. Will you autograph your book for me?" the nurse begged. She left the room and returned one moment later with a large and very well read paperback.

"Do sign it," Margaret coached her, "remember, just write Silver Jamison Lake."

Without understanding why, Shelby awkwardly accepted the paperback. She held the book dumbfounded, not quite sure how to proceed. Still too numb to protest, she simply took the pen the nurse offered her. Mechanically she opened the flap.

Maggie moved closer to her. "Just write Silver Jamison Lake."

Shelby took the pen wondering if she were breaking any laws by impersonating a romance novelist.

"Oh this is wonderful," the nurse squealed as she wrote out that ridiculous name.

Who give their child such a preposterous name she thought returning the book and the pen back to the nurse.

"Have you met Mr. Romance, Andrei Claude? I swear he is the handsomest man alive. I heard he has a new movie coming out. I can't wait to see it!"

Clearly annoyed, the doctor pressed his lips together in displeasure. "Now that's quite enough, we have a young lady here I need to see too. Jack, Maggie, do you mind waiting outside for a few minutes?"

"Not at all, "Jack said as he ushered his mother out of the room.

Without another word, Jack and Maggie left the room. Didn't anyone notice Maggie Colter's behavior was odd, Shelby wondered. But then, at the moment, Maggie was the only one besides herself who knew she wasn't Silver Lake.

"Now young lady, I want to see you wiggle your fingers and toes."

Twenty minutes later, she emerged from the office holding a prescription in her hand.

"Silver, it's been decided," Maggie greeted her, "I insist that you come home with me. Jack is going to get your prescription filled and bring it to my house. Now, not another word, I insist!"

Jack looked as through he wanted to comment but Maggie gave him a gentle push toward the door.

"Run along Jack," Maggie insisted. "Silver and I will be going straight home. We need to chat. Do some girl talk. Get her settled at the house."

This had gone too far, Shelby thought, ready to voice the truth.

As if sensing Shelby was about to confess, Maggie's eyes widened. She wrapped her arm about Shelby's shoulder. "Silver dear, we can send for your things at the hotel later. Jack, Silver's head must be throbbing, please get to the drug store and hurry back. Doctor Edwards, just put her charges on my bill."

The doctor nodded and to Shelby said, "I'd like to check on you in a few days. Call my nurse for a time."

Jack took the prescription. "Okay, I'll be back as soon as I can. You'll be safe with my mother."

Shelby smiled. She wasn't so sure.

However, she kept her silence until she and Maggie were alone in Maggie's maroon sedan.

"He likes you!" Maggie squealed. "I knew he would!"

Exasperated, Shelby cried, "Mrs. Colter!"

"Now I thought we agreed you were going to call me by my first name?" Maggie said sweetly. She appeared quite unruffled by Shelby's sharp glare. "I can see you're angry with me but I had to come up with a story for you."

"You could have just told the truth!"

"Certainly not!" Maggie argued. "Besides, Jack likes you."

"Which is the point, Maggie, he trusts me to be who I am. You, we, I should tell your son the truth the minute he comes home."

"Oh, no!" Maggie said, "Jack mustn't know I have hired you to follow him. By the way, noticed anyone following him? Anything to report, well, besides almost getting killed outside his house? And Shelby dear, I'm sure it was an accident."

Shelby's head began to pound all the while wondering if Maggie was trying to change the subject. Regardless, she gave Maggie the truth, "Yes. While I haven't seen any direct evidence, a police officer who works for me during his off duty time noticed a truck passing by your son's house late last night. We're running the tags today."

Maggie pulled her car into the driveway just beyond Jack Colter's home. Shelby noticed her Tracker was still parked undisturbed across the street.

"You didn't tell me you lived next door to Jack."

"Didn't I?" Maggie replied innocently. Shelby almost

laughed and wondered what else she had neglected to mention. "You see when the house next door went up on the market a couple of years ago, I brought it for Jack. He was living in an apartment across town. Let me tell you, I had a terrible time convincing him to move in. I'm growing older and of course, one day Jack will want to get married. I'll be close to my grandchildren."

Shelby shook her head. How could anyone be so endearing and maddening at almost the same time? Still, in her own fashion, her intent was to protect her only son. Shelby had to respect Maggie for that.

"Shelby, there's no harm in pretending to be someone you aren't for a few days. You call that sort of thing undercover, right? And of course, by staying with me, you can see Jack all the time."

Shelby took a long breath. "Maggie, I need to follow your son, not be a part of his life."

Maggie was smiled and ignored Shelby's quiet statement. Her eyes were lit, filled with excitement as she parked the car behind her house.

"This will give you the perfect opportunity to keep a close eye on Jack," Maggie cooed happily. "And, It'll only be for a few days, you said so yourself. Oh, I just remembered, I should've told Jack to pick up my heart medicine while he was at the pharmacy."

"You need heart medicine?" Shelby asked as they got out of the car.

"Don't look alarmed. Doc Edwards says as long as I take my medicine, I'll be just fine. I do think you should do as the doctor said and get a bit of rest."

When they reached the back door, Maggie twisted the key unlocking the door. She stepped back and allowed Shelby to enter.

As Shelby entered the kitchen, Maggie asked, "Did you notice the way Jack looked at you? I just know you are the right girl…"

Shelby stopped and looked inquisitively at Maggie. What did she mean 'the right girl'?

Maggie blushed. "Did I say the right girl? I meant the right detective. Now just follow me. I know you want to lie down."

Shelby had little to do but to follow Maggie through her home.

Her house, like Jack's, must have been built in the late 1920s, though her kitchen had been thoroughly modernized.

The gray kitchen tile was easy to walk on and Shelby guessed there was extra padding beneath it. Sparkling pots hung above a sleek ceramic stove in an island in the center of the room. The conventional oven, microwave, and refrigerator were built in around the oak cabinets. Aside from the modern conveniences the kitchen held a quaint charm given to it by small souvenirs, memories, vacations spent, and an odd assortment of handmade clay bears and animals. Made by Jack perhaps? Yes, Maggie seemed the sort to keep such treasured gifts.

The Royal Dalton China set was not new and its timeless beauty was displayed in a spectacular glass cabinet. An array of red, green, and blue glass bowls that probably once belonged to a beloved aunt or grandmother fit comfortably among the dinner set right next to a crystal sugar and cream set.

The breakfast nook just off the kitchen looked at a spectacular English garden.

Shelby knew the difference between a house and a home and Maggie's Victorian spoke of decades of memories and love.

"Of all the rooms in my house," Maggie said softly, "I think I always like the kitchen best."

Shelby smiled.

Maggie looked beyond the place Shelby stood to the past. Her brown eyes grew misty as she said, "Though Jack was an only child, this old house was always filled with the sound of children laughing. I miss that."

"Well," she said, snapping back to the moment. "Let's find you a bed to rest in, Shelby. Jack should be here any minute with your medicine. Come on; follow me upstairs, I have just the room for you."

Shelby followed Maggie through the dining room with its magnificent antique oak table with matching serving board down a short hallway to the living room, which was filled with heavy sofas and chairs, bookcases, knickknacks, and memories of a family who had gathered in this room for many celebrations and gatherings.

With her head beginning to pound, Shelby would have liked to enjoy the house, but a large, heavy, grandfather clock chimed the hour as she passed.

Bordered by heavy brass decorative weights, the pendulum swung relentlessly behind the bright crystal clear door. Shelby grabbed her head to ward off the assault of chimes which filled the house with their ring.

She hurried up the long flight of stairs after Maggie, promising herself a closer study of a collection of family photos hung against the stair wall.

On the second floor, Maggie passed several closed doors to stop before one.

"This will be your room while you are staying here, dear," she said softly as she opened the door. Maggie crossed the room and pulled down the covers on the four poster bed. She moved quickly to the window and opened it allowing the fresh morning breeze and sweet scents of her flower garden to blow in.

The bed with the soft lavender canopy was inviting. The matching curtains and two high back chairs sat before a fireplace. The wallpaper was speckled with sweet little lilac flowers on short emerald stems.

The same pattern was repeated on the downy comforter. A sheer white material graced the canopy. Both the head board and foot board were fashioned into a lovely fan design. A breathlessly sheer white linen sash draped across the canopy's top almost falling on the bed's two oversized pillows. It was perfect and inviting.

"This room is beautiful," Shelby said, complementing her hostess. "Thank you."

Maggie carefully folded back the comforter. "My darling, I want you to lie down. I'll bring you a cup of tea later. You banged your head pretty bad."

"I should go," Shelby protested, but her head was throbbing. "I shouldn't be putting you out this way."

"Nonsense, Jack will be back from Carter's Drug Store at any minute. He'll be suspicious if you aren't here. Besides, you need to rest. Now, not another word. You're staying here. I'll be back to check on your shortly."

Longing for a shower and her own bed just across town, it was simply easier to lie down in this strange but welcoming room than argue further with Maggie.

Shelby pulled off her running shoes and heard them drop to the floor. She was asleep before her head hit the pillow.

Glancing at her watch, it was close to noon when she woke. Still groggy, she couldn't believe she had slept so long. She decided a couple of aspirins would soothe her aching body.

"Good, you're up," Maggie said as Shelby entered the kitchen fifteen minutes later. "I've made you some lunch, nothing fancy, just some good old fashioned stew. I want you to eat something nourishing."

The bright little breakfast nook was already set with plates, bowls, and a platter filled with homemade biscuits. The heavy scent of beef and carrots was irresistible.

Shelby remembered she hadn't eaten since last night and she was ravenous. A small white bag with her prescription was on the table next to a glass of apple juice. She frowned as she read Silver Lake.

Maggie served up the stew from a large crock pot and set it in front of her.

Struggling to twist off the child proof cap, Shelby asked, "By the way, who is this Silver Lake anyway?"

"She's a very famous romance novelist. A dear friend introduced me to her writing a couple of years back and I've become a huge fan."

"If she is so well known, won't people know that I'm not her?"

"That's just it; no one has seen her. She prefers to live life in anonymity. One of those writer things, I suppose," Maggie said as the doorbell rang. "As I was saying, it was a family friend who insisted I read one of her books. I've been hooked ever since. Now, eat up, I'll get the door."

"Oh, this is wonderful, wonderful," Maggie squealed, returning to the room with a beautiful flower arrangement. Lifting the elegant white wicker basket in the air to show Shelby, it was filled with a spring bouquet of pink alstroemeria, lavender larkspur, white daisies, and a spray of pink rose buds.

Maggie helped herself to the card. "It's from Jack; he says he hopes you are feeling better. Oh, I knew he would like you the moment he saw you!"

"Maggie, about Jack..."

"Shelby, I know what you're going to say, but you only have to be Silver Lake for a few days."

"Maggie, please," Shelby pleaded. "While I have a relatively quiet social life and while most of my work is out of the limelight, there are still a lot of people who know me. I would hate for Jack to find out who I am without a proper introduction."

"Yes, I'd hate for that to happen too," Maggie agreed, wrinkling her brow. "We'll just have to take care that doesn't happen, won't we?"

Shelby didn't answer. She at last opened the cap and took two tablets as prescribed. While she ate, Maggie immediately began talking about happier times in her home.

Finishing the last of her stew, Shelby took the empty bowl to the kitchen sink. "Thank you very much for your hospitality, Maggie. But, I have to earn my keep. Can I help you with this?"

"Why don't you try to rest more, dear?" Maggie protested, "Jack will be at the store the rest of the day. I'm sure he'll be quite safe there."

Shelby tilted her head slightly and tried not to smile. "No, I really need to get back to work. I have to tell you I feel a bit guilty about all this. If you want a refund, I'll be happy to oblige you."

Maggie shook her head. "Nonsense. No harm done. My dear, you really should rest. You aren't leaving, are you?"

"I need to get back on track Maggie, and I need to change these clothes."

"But you'll be back later, right?" Maggie asked in a near whimper, "And you will stay the night here?"

"For tonight," Shelby reluctantly agreed. "Tomorrow is another day. We'll see. No promises beyond this evening, Maggie."

Before going home, Shelby drove back into downtown. She had to know that Jack was at the store. She was relieved to find his Bronco parked in front of the store.

She smiled, remembering the flowers he had sent that morning. For different reasons, she was finding the son almost as incorrigible as the mother. Perhaps he is just worried about her claiming damages against him.

Stopping at the red light just below Bear Creek Outfitters, she turned her head to notice Jack Colter stepping out of the bookstore. He paused no more than five feet from the bookstore. To her horror, she watched him reach deep into the bag and pull out what appeared to be an oversized romance novel.

Silver Lake was embossed in large letters across the front of the book.

Shelby gasped. Her hands clammy, her mouth dry, she watched mesmerized by the scene. Jack began flipping through the pages only to pause midway through the book. His dark brow wrinkled as if he found something disturbing, then as he eagerly turned to the next page, a look of pleasure crossed his face. Jack Colter's broad grin widen as he continued to read. Shelby knew this wasn't good.

On the sidewalk, Jack smiled. He was stunned and had trouble reconciling the wholesome Silver Lake with the sensuous woman who hid her passion neatly between the lines of a romance novel. Where they one in the same?

He read on, unable to take his eyes away from the words. Was this woman capable of such exploding passion? If her intent was to captivate a reader, she had certainly gotten his attention.

Closing the book, he barely noticed a truck blocking his way across the busy street. He was too distracted by the beautiful Ms. Lake to care.

Shelby had watched him tuck the book back into the plastic bag. What had he read that left him with that silly lopsided grin on his face?

Shelby slid down into the seat. Grateful that a delivery truck pulled up behind her just moments before Jack Colter had crossed the street. Jack was so absorbed in the novel, he hadn't even noticed she was there.

Her senses hit defcon five. She'd better get her hands on that Silver Lake book!

The light turned green. Spying an empty parking space three cars up, Shelby maneuvered the Tracker in-between two vehicles. With a quick glance up the street, Jack was out of sight, presumably he had returned to Bear Creek Outfitters.

She reached around in the back seat and slipped the baseball cap on her head. Tucking her brown hair under the cap, she pulled it low over her face. Satisfied, she left the Tracker and scooted along the store front half expecting Jack to jump out at her before she reached the book store.

"Hey Shelby," the sales clerk greeted her. "What are you in the mood for? The Shelley Wright book you were asking about is here."

"Great," Shelby said weakly, "but actually I think I'm in the mood for a good romance. What do you recommend, Carol?"

"Really?" Carol asked, popping her gum in her mouth. "You want a romance? No blood and guts, serial killers, or true crime? Well, okay, this way."

Shelby ignored the less than inquisitive look that crossed Carol's face. A frequent shopper, this was the first time she had ever asked for a romance. Carol waved her to follow and padded her way to the back of the store to the romance section.

Scanning for the author's name, the hollow pit in Shelby's stomach became an ache.

"If you like hot, steamy romances, you might want to read something by Silver Lake. We can't keep her books stock," Carol said, passing her a thick, glossy romance. "This is her latest, *Love's Passionate Dawn Reborn*. It's been selling like hot cakes."

Shelby looked at the cover. The knot in her stomach grew. Her mouth went dry. She wasn't sure she could swallow as she read in gold embossed print Silver Jamison Lake. The name dominated the book's cover. Shelby swallowed hard. It was her name, well, the writer she was impersonating name. Holding Silver Lake's book everything seemed too very real. She was almost certain this was the very book Jack Colter had been reading. How could she know for sure, they all looked the same?

Directly below the name, a half-clad buxom blonde stood back to back with a large bare-chested Scottish highlander. Both were clutching swords. The blonde's sword was slightly smaller, more feminine looking. The heroine's dress was torn at just the right angle to expose a long, slender leg.

It was locked against the muscular thigh of the hero. Her long blonde hair was streaming as if wind swept. Interesting, she thought, nothing else was affected by the wind. Considering the portions shown on the man this was probably a good thing.

Shelby surmised by the sizable medallion on his kilt that he was some sort of Scottish Lord. Behind them, smoke was billowing high into a dark sky. Presumably their castle under attack, and the couple was obviously ready for action. If Jack

Colter was reading this, she'd best prepare for a little action of her own.

Her eyes widened as they followed Carol's direction to a treasure cove of Silver Jamison Lake's novels. The saucy titles alone made her knees weak.

Carol nonchalantly smacked the gum in her mouth and pointed to a second display shelf. "More over there. Pretty hot stuff."

"I'll take this one," Shelby said, hoping she didn't sound as desperate to Carol as she did to herself.

With her purchase in hand she hurried back to the Tracker. She began flipping through the pages glancing for a word of a phrase that would catch her eye. She stopped midway through the torrid romance and read,

"You are mine Heather, your heart, your soul!" Thor screamed crossing the room.

Grabbing her small frame, he swept her into his arms. Without permission, his large hands began to caress her breasts. His rough fingers slid sensually to her silky thighs before cupping her soft bottom.

"I hate you Thor!" Heather screamed. She began pounding her small fists against his chest. In rage, she screamed, "I'm Richard's wife!"

Shelby groaned, slamming the book shut.

"This is definitely not good," she said for no one to hear. She threw the book across the seat and sighed; she knew where the storyline was going and at the same moment knew Jack was reassessing his opinion of her. This would be hilarious if it were happening to someone else.

The passenger door opened, startling her. Chris Thompson jumped into the vehicle. With a knee jerk reaction, Shelby reached for her gun, remembering too late she didn't have it on.

"Scared you?" Chris said with a laugh.

Shelby lightly punched him in the arm. "Not funny, Thompson. I'll tell your wife!"

"I know," Chris said sheepishly, "my wife doesn't think I am funny either."

"What's up?" she asked, noticing Chris had inadvertently knocked the book off the seat to the floor of the Chevy. She had no idea why she felt the need to hide the novel. Nervously, she brushed a strand of hair from her face. She licked her lips knowing perfectly well she was acting guilty. Good grief, she thought, possession of a romance novel was hardly a crime. But, she reminded herself, she had yet to read the whole book.

"Remember the pick up truck I was telling you about?" Chris asked, watching a couple of kids playing tag down the busy street.

"Yes, the brown truck you saw last night."

"Turns out the license plates are stolen. I've already put an APB out for the truck but so far, no sign of it. How was your morning?"

Tenderly touching the bruise on her head, she replied. "Don't ask."

For the moment, the romance novel and the racy plot were forgotten. Perhaps there was someone following Jack Colter after all.

"I'll keep an eye out for the truck. By the way, are you available for tonight? And don't ask me how, I don't have time to explain, but I'll be staying the night with Maggie Colter."

Chris, who never seemed surprised by her revelations or requests, was busy adjusting the police radio on his shoulder. "Sure, I'm looking for all the overtime I can get in. By the way, partner, is there something I need to know and be aware of besides this truck?"

Shelby looked at some women passing by her vehicle. "I actually don't know. Maggie thinks someone is following her son but won't give me any more information. I don't know who or why and I don't think she does either. I also have a hunch that something is going on that she's not telling me about."

Chris grunted. "Well, I appreciate the extra work, new baby coming and all. Speaking of, I need to get back on duty. See you later?"

"You bet, thanks Chris."

Chris left the Tracker and closed the door, peering in at Shelby one last time. "Okay, I'll see you tonight."

Shelby sat up in her seat and adjusted the rearview mirror. Crime of any sort in sleepy little Hendersonville was rare. Still, she was beginning to feel uneasy. Why would a truck with stolen plates be cruising Jack's neighborhood? Something didn't feel right about any of this and she didn't like to feel out of control.

With Jack in the store, no sign of suspicious activity, she decided to take advantage of the moment to make a quick trip home for a shower and pick up a few things for an overnight stay at Maggie's. Jack would be safe enough until her return.

She drove across Hendersonville to Jump Back Mountain to her home. Set quietly atop a small butte, her home was a sanctuary far away from all the cheating hearts she followed. At night she had a picturesque view of Hendersonville. She appreciated the quietness of her mountain, its isolation and beauty.

There were several messages on her answering machine and she listened to them while she threw a few things into an overnight bag.

The first was a call from Emmett Smith; he had called asking if she had heard from Maggie Colter. A corporate client called requesting she do a couple of background checks on perspective employees, no rush, he had said, call him next week. The last message was from a man who suspected his young wife was cheating on him.

Some things never change, she thought as she washed off the street grime and shampooed her hair.

As the water cascaded down her body, her mind began to drift back to Jack. His face, his eyes were inescapable. The warm flow of water danced about her face and she found herself wondering if his lips would be as sweet, his touch as soft?

In the cool darkness of her shower, she remembered his dark blue eyes gazing at her. Would those tranquil pools of blue turn black with fury when he found out everything about her was a lie?

She was uncomfortable with Maggie's outrageous story no matter how inventive it seemed at the time, but there was little she could do about it. Maggie was, after all, her client. Jack Colter, she reminded herself, was not part of her life. In a week or two he would be gone.

Dreaming of him were stolen moments that could never be. She was not about to fall for any man ever again and she would never fall for Mr. Jack Colter.

Drying off, she tried to leave thoughts of Jack Colter alone, but they trailed after her like a soft fragrance, intoxicating and filling her raw senses with a longing she hadn't felt in years.

Applying her makeup, she looked at the woman in the mirror.

"You're a fool Shelby MacGregor," she told the reflection. With a fresh vow, she added, "I'll make quick work of this. This time next week, I won't even remember his face."

She packed a few things and drove back to Bear Creek Outfitters. Without understanding why, she was relieved to find his Ford Bronco still occupying the same parking space. A quick glance about revealed no mysterious brown truck.

Using her cell phone, she called her corporate client and told him she would be available for the background checks he needed. She left a message with Emmett Smith's secretary thanking him for the referral to Maggie Colter. She then called the husband who thought his young wife was cheating only to find out he had changed his mind. He wouldn't need her services after all; he apologized.

Shelby thanked him but could tell by the sound of his voice, he would be calling her again.

Denial, she thought, was one of the strongest of all human traits. Why, she wondered, do humans as a species cling so to love and its promise of fidelity? If we didn't, I'd be out of a job. A still small voice inside her mocked, you mean like you denying that you are attracted to Jack Colter.

Shelby bit her lip and stared out the window. She hadn't been attracted to a man in years. For a second time, she warned her heart; Jack Colter is not for you.

With little to do but wait for Jack to leave, she picked up, *Love's Passionate Dawn Reborn*. In the back of the book, she found Silver Lake's brief biography.

Silver Lake had written over twenty-two romance novels. She lived alone with her cats and was an accomplished pilot. Her favorite place to develop story lines was while flying her small plane. Shelby snorted knowing full well she couldn't pen a single poem if her life depended on it, and she was sure she wasn't the only private eye in the U.S. who was afraid of flying.

She read on. Silver was also a renowned chef, known primarily for whipping up her specialty, Cajun Cooking. In fact, Silver had written two cook books. The first was titled

Silver Lake's Louisiana Kitchen. The second book was titled *The Raging Cajun.*

Shelby smiled, well good for good ole Silver she thought without a moment of jealousy. She, on the other hand, couldn't boil water, but she was a crack shot with any type of firearm.

The good news was Maggie had been right. On short notice, Maggie couldn't have chosen a better identity. No photo adorned Silver's latest novel and the last paragraph of her bio said while she loved to hear from her fans, she preferred to live in obscurity with her cats and her plane. There was certainly little enough for Jack or anyone else to find out about the real Silver Lake. She was safe for the moment anyway.

Shelby shook her head and smiled. She was glad that she didn't have to live up to Silver Lake's long list of talents and accomplishments. Her job was to find out who was behind the wheel of that old Ford truck.

She drove back to Bear Creek Outfitters and tried to think of anything but her handsome charge.

Jack left his store. He made only one stop on his way home. He hurried into a small flower shop and emerged minutes later with a dozen yellow roses.

Watching him carefully lay the roses in the back seat, she felt her heart unexpectedly twist. A warning voice whispered in her head. This was, after all, what you wanted, right? Yes, she lied to herself. It was never easy to deny that sometimes she wanted someone to bring her flowers, someone to care. It will pass, she scoffed, a momentary bump in the road. She took a deep breath and tried to get back to business. Perhaps Jack had a girlfriend after all. Maybe that was his secret.

Maybe he was seeing a married woman and didn't want his mother to know. Maybe the man following him was the woman's husband, or yikes, another private eye. Wouldn't that be comical? She wished she wasn't so dammed suspicious of everyone but it was her job and she reluctantly acknowledged who she had become. It was a far safer and more realistic place to be.

Jack, however, had no secret rendezvous. He drove directly to his house.

The flowers he had stopped for were for her. Feeling her palms sweaty against the wheel of the Tracker, her analytical demeanor a moment ago had vanished into an unexpected feeling of pure delight. She shuddered inwardly at the mix of emotions that swept through her. While on one level this pleased her greatly, she hated the pleasure she couldn't afford to high cost of involvement with any man. She knew how this would turn out. She could trust no man in her life. Uneasiness was overcoming her cool control. How much more uncomplicated and safer this all would be if Jack had been having an affair with a married woman.

Why did the one man she was attracted to in years have to be good looking and single? She was going to have to solve this case, but fast.

Jack got out of his Bronco and went inside the back of his house. Shelby seized the moment to pull into Maggie's house. Thank God, the driveway was on the opposite side of the house.

Grabbing her overnight bag, she ran to the back door.

Sounding more like a co-conspirator than a client, Maggie held open the screen door. "Hurry, Jack just came home. Come quickly my dear."

Safely inside, Shelby turned to Maggie. "I'm not comfortable with all this deceit and frankly, I see no reason why we don't just tell Jack the truth."

"I don't think that is a good idea," Maggie stammered nervously. "By the way, since you were following him this afternoon,have you made any discoveries?"

Again Maggie skirted the issues. Shelby deposited the overnight bag on the kitchen table.

"Well, yes, we have made two discoveries, if you will, and I'm not happy with either one," came Shelby's quick response. "First, there may indeed be someone following Jack. An old brown truck has been seen in the neighborhood; now this may of itself be nothing, but it does have stolen plates. I can't be sure at this point if it has anything thing to do with you or your son."

For just the briefest of moments, Maggie looked genuinely surprised and then rallied from the bombshell. "Really? I'm sure not to worry, just a coincidence."

Shelby watched the older woman who seemed to just brush off the looming menace. There was no doubt this woman loved her only son, but why wasn't she more anxious about the truck and its occupants?

"Well, this is very odd indeed." Maggie brushed a stray gray curl from her face. Her face brightened and she smiled. "Well, I have a feeling Jack will be here momentarily. Anything else?"

Shelby took a deep breath. "Yes, I think there may be a bigger problem in the works. Jack bought several Silver Lake romance novels this afternoon. Maggie, we can't let this ruse go on."

"He did, did he?" Maggie squealed. "Oh my! This is wonderful. He must be interested in you, because he hasn't brought a book in years!"

Shelby felt her face color. "Maggie, this isn't a good thing and its another reason why Jack needs to know the truth."

"Not just yet," Maggie purred in a whisper, "We'll just keep this little secret between us for now. Trust me, Jack can take care of himself, so no sense in raising any alarm, that's my motto."

At that moment, Jack opened the screen door and Shelby grabbed her bag from the table hiding it behind her small frame.

Wordless, Maggie took the bag and dropped it quietly behind the counter.

"You're up? I thought you'd be resting," Jack said as he brought the long stemmed yellow roses from behind him. "These are for you. I had to admit, I'm feeling very guilty about the accident this morning."

An unwelcome blush burned its way across her cheek. Good heavens, she chided herself, the flowers were not a romantic gesture, just a considerate act by a man who was probably worried about his insurance rates. What had she been thinking? But more importantly, why? She was helpless to halt her embarrassment and looked down at the tile hoping no one would notice her shudder of humiliation. What a fool she was, after all this time, what an utter fool.

She knew he was waiting for a response.

"Jack," Shelby said awkwardly looking back to him. "I don't know what to say. Thank you. They are very lovely."

"Not half as lovely as you," Jack said with a smile. "You look much better than this morning."

Well, she thought, considering she was laying sprawled across the pavement fighting consciousness, she certainly hoped so.

"Here, I'll take them," Maggie offered. "I have just the perfect vase for roses."

"Thanks Maggie," Shelby faltered in what sounded like a girlie voice. What the heck is wrong with me, she chided herself, but to Jack she smiled and said, "Thank you for the flowers."

He grinned and it was both infectious and devastating. His eyes were gentle and contemplative. "How's your head?"

"Actually, except for a major headache this morning, I haven't had any problems the rest of the day."

"Good, I'm glad to hear that."

Jack reached out and touched her hand giving it a slight squeeze. The heavy lashes that showed her cheeks flew up. As his fingers touched hers, a sudden tingling rose from within her spreading its dancing fire throughout her body. He was standing so close she could taste his breath.

Jack's warm, blue eyes never left her. He seemed unaware of his effect on her. In a sensual velvet voice he said in a near whisper, "I'm genuinely glad you are better."

Watching her, Jack was again smitten by her melting loveliness. She was slender, athletic, and he found the slight blush to her face charming. A writer, a business woman, a pilot, and an accomplished chef, she was just too good to be true.

From the tip of her pretty Grecian nose to her dark brown hair with glowing auburn highlights, she was beautiful, and despite the circumstances of how they met, he couldn't believe his good fortune. He knew to take things slow, not to rush, not to frighten her off, but he also had to admit he was interested in the woman who stood before him.

His mother interrupted his thoughts.

"Dinner is almost ready," Maggie said, drawing both Shelby's and Jack's attention.

Maybe it was the wild glint in Maggie's eye or the peculiar curve of her smile. Perhaps it was the way Maggie tilted her head shyly or the mischievous good girl gone bad look, but Shelby sensed something horrible was about to happen. She didn't have to wait long to find out.

"Jack, as you may or may not know, our Silver is an accomplished gourmet cook."

Oh no, no, Shelby protested, trying to signal Maggie to stop. Maggie continued on as though she was hunted by the hounds of hell.

"In spite of her injury, Silver insisted on getting up and making us a fabulous dinner. Pun intended, she literally wrote the book, two of them as a matter of fact. Instead of resting as Dr. Edwards suggested, she insisted on whipping up one of her favorite Cajun meals. Jack, tonight we're being treated to New Orleans black muffins, served with chicken and seafood jambalaya, candied sweet potatoes, and fresh sautéed vegetables. You will of course, stay for dinner."

Shelby turned sharply toward Maggie. She should have liked at that moment to inform her client that she could barely scramble eggs!

"To top it off, "Maggie continued brightly, "she baked the most delicious apple sweet dough pie I've ever seen. If it tastes half as good as it smells, we're in for some real tasty treats."

"An apple pie!" Shelby repeated, but no one seemed to notice the rise in her voice. "Now I baked an apple pie!"

Jack could do little more than stare at this utterly amazing woman! Surely she wasn't feeling that well from the morning's fall but she had taken it upon herself to get up out of bed and prepare a magnificent meal. He was flattered.

With a soft and appreciative smile, he agreed. "Of course, I will stay for dinner. My mother must have told you, I love apple pie."

"But I…that is…"

"Jack, this poor little thing has been in the kitchen all afternoon. Please take her to the sofa; I'll finish up in here. It's the least I can do."

"This way, Silver, lets get you off your feet. Mother, can I help with anything?"

"No, no, just entertain Silver, if you would," Maggie said with an impish smile.

With a hard glare at Maggie, which the older woman ignored, Shelby followed Jack into the living room and sat down at one end of the sofa. Feeling very annoyed with Maggie and the situation, it would serve Maggie right if she confessed everything to Jack right now, but she never broke her word with a client, no matter how inviting the moment seemed.

"Could I interest you in a glass of wine?" Jack said, going to the small bar at the end of the sitting room.

"Actually," Shelby replied, wondering exactly how much alcohol was in the Colter house. She might need it before this assignment was through. "Thank you Jack, a small glass of white wine would be nice."

Jack brought a glass of white wine and raised his bourbon and water,

"I'd like to propose a toast."

Accepting the wine, she weakly raised the glass dreading what he was about to say next.

Jack watched the shy way she brought the glass to her lips. Her perfectly formed mouth was proving to be a distraction, and the long, dark lashes that shadowed her pretty blue eyes were thick and natural. Once again he was lost in her eyes.

"To a lovely and talented lady," he announced cheerfully as he raised his glass to hers, "may this night be the first of many."

Shelby smiled and drowned the wine in a single gulp. Looking up to him meekly she held the empty glass in her hand. Great, he probably thinks I am an alcoholic.

Jack took a seat across from her. "I went out and bought some of your books this afternoon. You're quite the writer."

Shelby shifted uneasily in her seat. The passage she had read came back to her word for word. She hoped he didn't notice her hands were shaking.

"Do you mind if I ask you a personal question," he said, leaning toward her. Shelby shook her head. "Good, and I hope you won't think me forward; you are single, right? No man in your life?"

"No," she said out loud, then to herself, well except for the off duty married policeman I have following you, there is no man in my life. Playing with the empty glass in her hand, she looked at him and added, "Jack, I'm not the person you think I am."

"You're right about that!" Jack agreed too quickly. "Your books were..."

"Exciting," Shelby finished for him knowing full well that wasn't the word he was looking for. With as much dignity as she could muster, she added, "You shouldn't judge a book by the cover."

Jack laughed. Shelby grimaced. Wrong answer.

"I'm sorry," Jack apologized, noticing the empty glass in her hands. "Let me get you another one."

He took the empty glass and headed toward the bar.

As he refilled her glass, he felt like an awkward teenager on his first date saying all the wrong things. In his attempt to make small talk, he was stumbling all over himself.

Returning the glass to her, he said, "I apologize, I didn't mean to suggest you...well, that is, your books are. Geeze, I'm making matters worse."

"Its okay," Shelby said, embarrassed by the discussion, "just because I write about that stuff doesn't mean I..."

She stopped, he grinned.

Quickly changing the subject, or attempting to, he took another track. "So, how did you get involved writing romances?"

Actually, your mother came up with this ridiculous story so that I could follow you, Shelby wanted to say, but instead she said to him, "I always wanted to be a writer. Jack, I would rather learn more about you."

Jack sat down, relaxed, and took a sip of his drink. "There is nothing at all exciting about me, Silver. I'm my father's son, born and raised right here in this very house. After college, I went into the family business, and unfortunately when my father passed away, I took it over."

"What brings you to Western North Carolina? Seems like I remember my mother saying you were doing research on a book."

Shelby nodded; she had at last found an answer that wasn't a lie. "Yes, you could say that, I'm doing research."

Jack waited for her to elaborate, she obliged. "I thought Hendersonville would be a perfect setting for a novel. So, I'm taking in the sights."

"Well no one knows this area better than me," Jack offered, "I'd love to show you around."

Before Shelby could answer Maggie walked into the room carrying a heavy tray of shrimp appetizers.

"Now that is an excellent idea!" Maggie said with delight. "Dinner is just about ready and Silver, I know you probably wanted to do the ceremonies but I couldn't wait. I knew you wouldn't mind me bringing these goodies in."

Before setting down the platter of shrimp in front of them, she gave the delicacies a full 180 degree turn to show them off. "Look, this is garlic shrimp, barbeque shrimp, and coconut beer-battered shrimp with sweet and tangy dipping sauce."

Jack reached out for a coconut battered shrimp and popped it in his mouth, "This is delicious!"

"Why don't you have one too, Silver?" Maggie offered sweetly.

Incensed, Shelby could do little but glare at Maggie. Maggie popped another shrimp into her mouth and grinned shamelessly.

"Where exactly do you live in Louisiana?" Jack asked, getting a second helping.

The shrimp, with its light flavor, seemed to melt in his mouth. Man, this woman could cook! "Mother, Silver and I were getting acquainted. May I ask exactly where you live? Seems like I read somewhere in Arcadia, I believe."

"I'm not sure," Shelby muttered, still too furious with Maggie to think clearly. Jack's blank look brought her back to the moment. She added quickly, "I meant that I'm not sure where I live anymore, flying around the county to book signings and publishers' meetings."

Jack nodded, satisfied with her answer.

"Well, Hendersonville is a quiet little town, a good town to settle in," Maggie said, then added quickly, "and raise a family."

Shelby sank into the chair and let the conversation flow around to the family business. Jack told Maggie about the some shipments that went out to the wrong retailer that he was able to correct.

Shelby was lost in thought when Maggie caught her attention.

"I think that is a wonderful idea, Jack! Silver, don't you agree?"

Shelby looked at Maggie then to Jack. "I'm sorry, what did you say?"

Maggie was beaming. "Jack was telling me he was going to show you around Hendersonville for your book's research. I think that is a wonderful idea!"

Under the circumstances, she could do little but agree.

"Great," Jack said, "I'm due a few days off from the store. I can certainly take the time to drive you around. By the way, what is your book about? Another historical romance?"

"No," Shelby replied, she said glaring straight at Maggie Colter, "this is more of a contemporary book about a private investigator who winds up in a real pickle."

"Sounds interesting. Do you know any real private eyes?"

"As a matter of fact, I do," Shelby replied, throwing a menacing look to Maggie.

"Well, let's not keep that delicious dinner waiting another minute," Maggie said, rising to her feet. Shelby couldn't help but admire Maggie's gift of easing out of tight situations. Shelby speculated that if Maggie hadn't chosen the life of a housewife and mother, she would have made a great career criminal.

Everyone stopped at the dining room entrance. Every inch of space on the table was filled with plates and platters of Cajun cuisine. Spicy aromas filled the entire room and each dish looked more delightful and more beautiful than the one before.

"Oh my gosh!" Jack and Shelby said in unison. Jack recovered first.

"You're a woman of many talents, Silver," he said, holding her chair out for her.

Only Maggie heard Shelby's soft growl as she sat.

Seated his mother, Jack wasted no time reaching for one of the muffins. "So, Silver, how is it a man hasn't snatched you up by now?"

"One almost did," Silver replied, accepting the basket of muffins, "but that was years ago. And thankfully, so is he."

Jack's eyes softened. "I'm sorry. Years ago I lost my heart to someone too. She betrayed me, lied to me. It took me years to get over her. In fact, while I can't remember her face anymore, I remember how it felt to be lied to."

"Let's not talk about sad times, Jack," Maggie quipped, offering him a platter of sautéed vegetables. The aroma of the food was intoxicating.

"This is truly a wonderful meal, Silver, "Jack said, his plate filled with the entrees. "You're one amazing woman. Is there nothing you can't do?"

Shelby smiled not knowing what to say.

They finished the meal with light chatter.

She had to remind her heart more than once that under no circumstances would she, could she, let his handsome, debonair man into her life. Years of investigative work had left her with one and only one conclusion; no man would ever be trusted.

She had to keep a cool distance and a cool head if she was going to do her job. And, she acknowledged, she had to get Jack Colter out of her life as soon as possible.

Watching the casual way he moved, sultry, masculine, she knew those dark, mysterious, sea blue eyes would surely be the death of her. She couldn't help but notice the tenderness that he showed his mother. Breathlessly aware of this man, she knew under other circumstances she might have even enjoyed his light flirtation.

Still, Shelby was wistfully aware of the strong sense of family in the room. Despite everything past, everything present, everything future, she wished somewhere, somehow she could be part of so much love. Taken unaware by her own heart, she realized she had been alone too long.

As the meal concluded, Shelby realized she was developing a strong fondness with Maggie and her silly, bizarre, elaborate schemes. To be honest, she also had to acknowledge a very strong attraction to Jack Colter. Clearly, she was on dangerous ground.

Maggie sliced the sweet dough apple pie, and cut three slices. She first passed a slice to Shelby, then to Jack before serving herself.

The doorbell rang. Its sound resonated through the old house in sharp alarm. Call it feminine intuition, years of police force, or maybe it was her time spent in private investigations, Shelby knew this case was suddenly going from bad to worse.

CHAPTER THREE

Look who's here," Maggie said, returning with a large, burly, white-haired man in tow. "Brad McClannahan." Shelby looked at him and was greeted with an instant warm, friendly smile. Though he stood 6' 4" and must have weight close to 250 lbs. Shelby instinctively knew he was one of those gentle giants who despite his size wouldn't hurt a soul. His silvery blond hair, fair skin, and strong, angular jaw spoke of a Dutch or German ancestry, and his deep blue eyes were sparkling with laughter.

She dismissed her premonition, this man was no threat to her, or was he? Her instincts were very rarely wrong.

"Now where did this pretty little thing come from?" Brad said. The warmth of his voice filled the room.

"Actually from your neck of the woods," Jack replied. "She's from Bayou country. You can't have her, after this delicious meal, I've claimed her. She's mine."

Brad laughed. "Jack, you know your mother is the only woman for me. For five years I've been asking her to marry me she still won't say yes!"

Maggie giggled and managed a school girl blush. "Brad, you're a big tease. Now do hush up so I can make proper introductions. Dear one, Brad is one of our oldest and dearest friends. He's part of the family. And Brad, I'd like you to meet the famous romance novelist, Silver Jamison Lake!"

Brad's blue eyes narrowed and grew dark. His relaxed

pose stiffened. His face changed from warm benevolence to one of shock then pure animosity.

"Silver Lake?" was all he could manage. "The romance novelist, Silver Lake?"

Shelby knew instinctively something was very wrong. Brad continued to glare at her. Neither Jack nor Maggie seemed to notice the change.

"You're just in time for pie," Jack said, motioning the older man to join them at the table. "Now I know how you pride yourself on your Cajun cooking, but this little lady wrote the book, in fact two on Louisiana cooking."

Brad scanned the table. His light blue eyes widened with fury as he took in the chicken and seafood jambalaya, candied sweet potatoes, and sautéed vegetables before resting on the New Orleans black muffins.

Shelby had never seen food have such a negative reaction on anyone before.

She began running his name and his face through her memory. Had she crossed paths with this massive man before? Certainly she would have recognized a client. Had he been a paramour of one of her client's spouses? Perhaps he was a criminal from her days with the police department. For the moment, she was unable to place him. On the other hand, he seemed to know her.

Watching Brad moved slowly about the table, he never once took his eyes off Shelby. Settling in the chair across from her, his eyes remained fixed on her.

"So you are the famous author, Silver Lake," he repeated with a sneer, "imagine that."

Shelby half smiled. So he wasn't one of Silver Lake's fans. He didn't have to be so nasty.

"Silver, Brad is one was the one who introduced me to your books," Maggie cooed. "Brad, really this pie is simply delicious. In fact it's Silver's signature dessert. Do have a slice."

"You baked this sweet dough apple pie?" Brad growled. "So, Ms. Lake, what brings a famous novelist like you to our little mountain town."

"Silver's doing research on a book," Maggie interjected, and then sounding very pleased added, "Jack has offered to show her around."

Jack nodded and looked straight at the older man. "Say, Brad, could we talk you into taking Silver up in your Cessna Cub? I'm sure she'd enjoy a bird's eye view of the mountains."

Shelby leaned back, uncomfortable with the direction this conversation was headed. She had no intention of getting into a plane with this man. The way he was looking at her, he would probably throw her out the plane at 15,000 feet.

"That's a great idea, Jack," Brad said with an even smile. Turning to Shelby he added, "How about it, Ms. Lake? I understand you've been flying for quite a while."

"That's so nice of you, Brad," Maggie cheered, adding her voice to the fray.

"I wouldn't want to impose on Brad," Shelby protested. She didn't want to admit she was afraid of flying and small planes terrified her. However, at the moment, Brad McClannahan was her biggest worry. Who was he? Why was he so angry with her?

"She's all mine tomorrow," Jack announced, looking tenderly at Shelby. "I suppose I could bring her by Thursday or Friday."

"Perfect," Brad sneered.

Shelby cringed. No one seemed to notice his open hostility but her.

Something was amiss and she didn't know what. She also knew that she had two, possibly three days before the truth would come out. When it did, the Colters and this Brad McClannahan fellow would be out of her life for good.

"Try some dessert, Brad," Maggie said, slicing him a huge piece of the apple dough pie.

Brad looked at the pie as if it was filled with toxins. He shook his head and returned his steady, even glaze back to Shelby. "No thanks, I just finished a big meal up at the lodge, Maggie, but I'll take some of your coffee."

"Absolutely, Brad," Maggie said with a smile, then to Jack said, "It's a lovely evening. Why don't you take our little Silver out to enjoy the garden? She could use some fresh air."

Ready to get away from Brad McClannahan, she would have gone with the devil, but Jack Colter was certainly a more attractive and preferable choice.

"You kids run along," Maggie insisted, "I'll take care of this later."

Shelby was just outside the room, when she heard Maggie say, "She's such a sweet girl."

"Maggie," Brad said in a low angry whisper. "Do you know anything about this girl? You can't just let anyone into your home. I swear woman, if you had a brain in your head..."

Maggie's light laughter covered the rest of his warning.

Jack had already crossed the kitchen and was waiting for her to join him. Though she had seen the garden by day, she was hardly prepared for the beautiful outdoor world Maggie had fashioned in the moonlight.

Filled with flat river stones that curved their way through a thicket of rose bushes, it wound past several antique birdbaths to stop at a small white gazebo in the far corner. It was midsummer night and the garden was alive and in full bloom. A sweet smell of perfumed lilies and honeysuckle hung in the air, a thick fragrant mist that layered the garden in magical, honeyed aromas.

The Carolina moon was a massive golden sphere that had just risen above a stand of oaks. It bathed the garden in soft ivory light. Though the garden was alive with vibrant color by day, at night the garden was brilliant in silvery foliage and pale shades that delicately picked up the luminescent glow of the moon. Several four-foot high trellises were draped in vines and moonflower. This was a quiet world, a world away from all others. It had been designed for romantic strolls and peaceful moments below the starry night sky.

Shelby turned but almost fell into Jack's chest. His arms gathered naturally around her. Her nearness was overwhelming.

A surge of wanting ran through him and he couldn't deny the spark of excitement at the mere prospect of a stolen kiss.

She felt small and light in his arms. She had captivated him. He wanted her to find him desirable, as irresistible as he was finding her.

"Look at the moon," she said trying to turn away, but he held her with such gentleness she dared not move. She was both breathless and shy. Her heart was racing. She dared not look up into his eyes. "It's absolutely beautiful. Perhaps we should go and ask your mother to come out."

"Not just yet, Silver," he said in a soft whisper. Her closeness was intoxicating. He tenderly began to explore her with his eyes, going places he wanted to touch with his lips.

Jack's fingertips were feather-light, soft, and sensual as he traced them gently across her shoulders. His arms wrapped about her. His breath was warm, sweet, and succulent as it danced lightly across her face. His index finger gently lifted her chin as if not to frighten her. Only a breath separated his firm lips from hers. Shelby looked up; Jack's blue eyes were warm with hunger, and yet strangely reflective. In his arms, she felt exhilaration, fear, and safe. She was too close to him. She couldn't bear the intensity of the moment.

With an awkwardness she hadn't felt since her teens, she placed her hand on his broad chest. Pressing it lightly against him, she pushed away. Jack offered no resistance. Shelby looked across the garden. Standing not six inches away from him, she already missed his nearness. In a voice that was barely audible, she asked, "Who is Brad?"

"He was my father's best friend," Jack explained. He wasn't ready for her to slip out of his arms. Though disappointed, he managed to have the good manners to let her go, at least for the moment. He cleared his throat and answered her, "My dad met Brad in the army. Two southern boys, they became great friends. He spent most of his life in New Orleans and moved here after the mess with Katrina. Between you and me, I think he has been in love with my mother all his life."

"And what about her?"

"My mother? Ha! The only thing on her brain these days is grandchildren. Suddenly," he added with a wicked grin, "I'm in the mood to oblige her."

Shelby blushed. She looked across the garden trying to focus on the gazebo. Jack was watching her, and he knew she was smiling.

"So, how come you aren't married with kids?" she asked boldly.

"Me?" Jack asked as if she had taken him by surprise. "I love kids. Would love to have a house full, just never met the right woman. What about you?"

"Never met the right man."

Jack grinned and came up behind her. He gently placed her small hand on the crook of his arm. He felt the electricity of her touch. Did she feel it too?

"Come, let me show you the gazebo," he said in a hushed tone.

Together they strolled down the path. The moment was too perfect. Deep within, she felt her heart racing the moon. She relished each moment so near to him, yet she knew she was walking on dangerous ground.

"So what specifically are you researching?" Jack asked, breaking the quiet of the garden.

"Just gathering information for a location of my new book," Shelby lied. How easy it is becoming for me to lie, she noted. She didn't find pleasure in this. Deciding it was best to cover her proverbial tracks she added, "I really don't like to talk about my work in progress."

The conversation was becoming even more precarious by the moment. If she was going to manage the situation and Jack, she would have to control their activities. She absolutely could not run the risk of running into someone she would know or would know her. Where could they go?

"If your offer is still open, I haven't seen the Blue Ridge Parkway," she suggested, "that is of course, if it's not too much trouble."

Jack paused and looked down at her. "Well, if you are up for it, we could take a short drive on the Parkway tomorrow."

"Good," she said with a smile. It was midweek, few locals would be on the Parkway. She felt suddenly relieved.

"What time can I pick you up? And by the way, if my mother hasn't mentioned it, I live right next door."

"Yes, she mentioned it," Shelby replied. She was infinitely annoyed at Maggie for omitting that tidbit of information from Jack's profile. Did it matter? What troubled her more was the feeling Maggie was withholding some piece of information that would prove vital to the case.

"Eight will be fine," Shelby answered Jack as she wondering how she was going to keep her attraction to this man at bay.

The serenity of the garden and his closeness grew in intensity as if an unbreakable bond was forming between them. She wasn't sure she could manage this romantic setting with Jack one moment longer. Coward, she chided herself as she said, "Jack, if you don't mind, I think I will turn in for the night."

"I'll let you go Silver, "he promised softly, "but not before I do this."

His arms were suddenly about her. There was no escape for her this time, and she wasn't sure she wanted one. His soft mouth came down on hers and the sweetness of its warmth seared her lips.

Taken by surprise, she felt her arms rise to resist him but instead, of their own accord, her arms slid about his shoulders, pressing her body into the sweetness of his. She was lost in the ecstasy of his embrace; her body melted into his. The smell of him was intoxicating. Her mind, her heart, her soul was drowning in a flood of sweet pleasure.

All the while her mind was telling her to resist, her body refused, giving into his sweet kiss. Her heart hammered foolishly inside and a warm shiver of wanting ran through her. She tried to slow her pulse, she tried to pull away; she couldn't.

Perhaps it was the pull of the moonlight, or the overwhelming sense of emotion too deep, too real to grasp that at last pulled them apart.

"I'm not sorry for that Silver," he said, his voice was husky and sensual, and sent a ripple of awareness through her.

Still trembling at the unexpected surge of emotions, she stared at him. It was the good meal, it was the moon, it was anything but the magic that was growing between them; she tried to tell herself. Her heart was pounding, and she was too breathless to even speak.

He pulled her back into his arms and rocked her slowly. "I'm glad I didn't run you over this morning."

"Me too," Shelby said so softly she wasn't sure he had heard her voice. For one unguarded moment, she relaxed, this felt too right, too perfect, and yet so very, very wrong. This was a stolen kiss, it couldn't be anything more.

As if sensing she was about to pull away from him, his hand cupped her right shoulder. He stared with deep longing for something more than just a kiss. He was begging her not to go.

Fearing she was about to lose a part of her she could never reclaim, she fought the moonlight, the sweet smell of magnolias and honeysuckle. She fought for a foothold in reality away from him. The terror seized her, consuming her. If she were to survive this night, she had to run away from Jack Colter. She had to run away from her heart.

I cannot enter this safe warm place, she thought, brushing away a tear that threatened to fall. I will not, she cried to her soul. She knew too well, the dark side of love where hurt and pain hid in the shadows. With her whole body shaking, she knew she was standing on unholy ground.

"I have to go," she insisted. "It's late."

"Silver," Jack said, his voice soft. "Look, you've had an eventful day and I promise I won't look so dangerous in the morning."

Despite herself she grinned. With a laugh, she said trying not to sound coy, "I'm not so sure about that."

He brought his face close to her and with a broad grin said, ""Well, you'll have to get to know me and my mountains. You'll see this is a safe place. Now I forbid you to leave me alone in the moonlight. I'll walk you in and save my kisses for another time."

Damn, she cursed in silence, why was he always so charming, funny, and so handsome?

His hand came down to possessively cover her trembling fingers. Lifting her hand, he wrapped it on the inside of his elbow. His biceps were hard and his skin cool to the touch, and the heat emanating from his body was as intoxicating as the sweet garden flowers. There was nothing boyish about him and he moved with a commanding manner that was captivating.

She should have been angry at the kiss but instead it still warmed her lips and her heart. Ignoring his masculinity and his sweetness was going to be more difficult than she was willing to admit.

However, he was a man of his word and without further comment,, he walked her back to the house. When they reached the back step, he made no further attempt to keep her near him. Shelby wasn't sure if that pleased her or not.

"Going to bed, dear?" Maggie said when they returned to the living room. "You look tired, dear."

Shelby gave Maggie a nod. "Yes, I'm tired."

Despite the glare from Brad McClannahan, good manners dictated she at least address him. "Nice meeting you, Brad."

With that and a final smile and nod in Jack's direction, Shelby allowed Maggie to guide her toward the stairway.

"Good night, Silver," Jack softly called out to her. "Sweet dreams."

Shelby returned his smile and followed Maggie up the long flight of stairs.

Once inside the room, Maggie flipped on the bathroom light and pulled out a floral terry wash cloth and a large matching towel from the cupboard. She laid them on the bathroom counter.

Maggie wasted no time crossing the room to fold down the covers for her guest. "I'm glad you are here."

"Thank you," Shelby replied, "but I really think we need to tell Jack the truth."

"Not yet, Shelby dear," Maggie cooed, "let's give it a day or so. We'll have to come up with a plan to tell Jack in just the right way."

This was against her better judgment but Shelby had little choice.

"One more day," Shelby warned. Maggie's smile was a weak attempt of complacency and Shelby knew it.

Helping Maggie with the lavender quilt, Shelby said, "Jack and I are driving to the Parkway tomorrow. I doubt if I will run into anyone who knows me there, especially midweek. If there is anyone following Jack, I will be able to keep him safe."

"Good thinking," Maggie lauded her. "Oh, by the way, I smuggled your things in earlier. Your clothes are in the dresser. I put your gun in the nightstand."

This woman is incorrigible and without conscience, Shelby thought, hiding a wicked grin from Maggie. Maggie did not need further encouragement.

"You understand, Jack could find out the truth on his own at any time."

"But he won't be half as mad at you as he will be at me."

Shelby found no comfort in Maggie's words. She wondered if a man who appeared to be so slow to anger would prove indomitable when enraged.

Before she left the room, Maggie gave her a quick squeeze.

"Not to worry, these things happen to me all the time. Now have a good night's sleep."

Alone at last and too tired to think, Shelby managed a quick shower. She slipped into her comfortable, well-worn night shirt, and turned out the light.

The light breeze carried with it the still sweet smell of magnolias and summer flowers, but also something more, the soft mummer of voices directly below her in the garden.

In the darkness of the room, she walked across to the window. Just below her she could see the outline of Jack and Brad McClannahan talking to one another. She listened to their words.

"You don't know anything about this woman!" Brad argued.

"I know she is beautiful, talented, and interesting. Why are you so suspicious?"

"She's not who she says she is, Jack," came Brad's quick reply.

"Come off it Brad! Why would she lie?" Jack snapped, "Come up with something besides your feminine intuition and I'll listen. Until then, I'm planning on keeping company with the prettiest woman I have seen in this town in years."

"I'll find out who this Silver Lake is," Brad warned. "I don't know what her scam is, but I intend to find out. While you are out tomorrow, I'm going to do a little poking around myself. I want to know who this woman is and what she wants."

Shelby fell back into the soft sheer white curtains, wondering why Brad McClannahan was so suspicious of her. He apparently knew something, but what? With growing suspicions of her own, she wondered if Brad had something to do with the reason she was here. She decided to find out a little more about Brad McClannahan herself and why he was making such a fuss over her.

In the dark, it took her several minutes to find her cell phone. She dialed Chris Thompson.

"Hi Shelby," Chris answered on the first ring. "I'm right outside the house. Nothing has happened since Brad McClannahan left the Colter house a few minutes ago."

"You know Brad McClannahan?" Shelby asked in surprise.

"Sure, he moved here a while back. He volunteers with the Civil Air Patrol. He helped out last spring when we found those lost hikers. Heck of a nice guy."

"Not by me," Shelby protested. She filled Chris in on her accident that morning, the encounter with Jack, and the elaborate cover Maggie created for her. When she finished she could feel her cheeks burning. Chris didn't bother to hide his snickers. A split second later he burst into a roar of laughter.

"That's a good one! A romance novelist! That sounds like something Maggie Colter would come up with. Ha!"

"Well, it's not funny to me. Look, I am stuck in here, so keep me posted if anything comes up."

"You got that, Ms. Lake. Oh, oh, can I have your autograph, Ms. Lake?"

Shelby hung up the phone to the sound of his laughter.

Minutes later she was fighting with the covers and pillows, still feeling annoyed with Chris, Maggie, and herself. How and why had she let Maggie Colter talk her into this foolishness? Had she finally lost her mind?

The bed was comfortable and the night air was both cool and sweet. The four poster bed swallowed her in rich comfort. Shelby settled back into the soft pillows and tried not to think of Jack or his sweet kisses.

I was tired tonight and caught up in the moment, nothing more, she told herself with some sense of satisfaction.

Moving the pillow to better suit her head and neck, she closed her eyes. Despite her best effort to push Jack Colter from her mind, several long minutes' later weariness swept over her and she fell into a deep sleep dreaming about the strong feel of Jack Colter's arms around her.

CHAPTER FOUR

The next morning, Jack woke thinking about the pretty romance writer just next door. His memories of her were clear and he savored each moment spent with her. He'd gone to bed reading a few more passages of her book. Not only was she a gifted writer, but her sexual nature so blatantly laid down in paper spoke volumes, only sharpening his growing interest in her. No shame in that he thought as another round of memories of her swept over him. Good to know, he thought with a private chuckle, I'm not dead yet.

He rose up in bed slightly and folded his arms behind his head unable to believe his good luck. Silver Lake was the package. She was beautiful, successful, and talented, and man could she cook. He wondered if there was anything she couldn't do.

She's too good to be true, a cynical inner voice cut through his thoughts warning himself to not rush in too fast. In the darkness, he stretched and frowned, slightly willing the suspicious thoughts away. True, he argued with himself, she painted a beautiful picture, but he sensed there was something she was holding back from him. What? He'd seen it in her eyes and felt it in her kiss.

What was haunting her? Old love? An unexpected burst of jealously hit him hard in the stomach, and while he realized he was in the first throws of attraction with the pretty novelist, the thought of her in another man's arms left him annoyed.

While not a jealous man by nature, he acknowledged he was simply envious of the man who had come before him and kissed those pretty lips.

"Well, we'll see," he said aloud. Glancing at the clock, it was too late to go back to sleep and too early to get up; there was nothing to do. He remembered the book on the nightstand and flipped on the light. He almost laughed as he realized he was interested in the storyline and if the poor heroine was actually going to escape from, what was his name, Thor? Rooting for Thor he flipped on the light and reached for the book on the nightstand. He was intrigued with the storyline. He was intrigued by Silver Lake.

Finding the dog-eared page he had marked the night before, he was curious as to what lay in store for Heather in the next few pages. He settled back while Heather once again shunned the attention of her Viking captor. With a lopsided grin, he had the feeling; Thor would give him a roadmap to manage the little vixen next door.

"Good morning, dear," Maggie said, welcoming Shelby into the kitchen just after eight. Shelby was a bit surprised to find Jack was sitting beside his mother. He greeted her with a knowing smile. She tried to smile back but something about his expression told her he knew something that she didn't. She couldn't imagine what.

"Good morning," Jack said, folding and laying the newspaper beside him. He wore a dark blue shirt that brought out the fire in his ruggedly handsome face. She tried not to notice his curious expression. Something was afoot, she knew it.

"I hope you slept well last night?" Jack asked pleasantly enough as he reached for his coffee up. "I have to tell you your book kept me up last night."

Shelby stiffened in shock and glanced nervously at Maggie. "Oh, really?"

"I've been telling Jack what a wonderful author you are for years," Maggie boasted rightly. "Now, I've fixed us all breakfast this morning but Jack and I were hungry so we already ate. So pardon our bad manners, dear. I left your plate in the microwave, it should still be warm."

Surprised to realize she was being treated to a homemade breakfast, she sat at the table unused to being waited on. Maggie brought the plate to the table and brought a pot of coffee to the table. She poured Shelby a cup and warmed hers and Jack's cup.

"You should have woke me earlier," Shelby said, accepting the cup. "I didn't realize how late I slept."

"Nonsense," Jack said with a roguish grin. "We're on no set schedule today."

As his sensuous mouth curled into a wide smile, a devilish look came into his eyes. She stared wordlessly across at him. Remembering their kiss in the garden, she decided she would pack her gun on her after all.

Despite the heavy meal she had last night, she found herself ravenous this morning and attacked the scrambled eggs with a vengeance. She stirred nervously in her chair and once again felt the pang of her cooperation in this lie she was withholding from Jack. She should just tell him, she thought, taking a bite of the scrambled egg. What was holding her back? Well, besides her promise to Maggie.

With a quick glance at Jack, she brought a slice of toast to her lips and took a dainty bit. She saw the heart wrenching tenderness in his gaze. Trying to return his smile, she crunched on the toast feeling anything but attractive as she did so. She once again had the feeling when the truth came out, she and Maggie would awaken a sleeping giant.

"Oh, it's time to take my heart pills," Maggie said, springing from the table. She crossed the floor to the kitchen sink and brought a small container to the table and swallowed the two pills with her orange juice.

Shelby noticed the soft look Jack gave his mother and smiled at the exchange. This was a good man and a good son.

Her cell phone rang as she took a bite of bacon. It was Chris. Both Maggie and Jack watched her read the number.

"Ah, it's my...ah...agent," Shelby quipped, answering the call. How easy it was becoming to lie.

"Shelby," Chris spoke without preamble, "I saw the truck again this morning around 4:30. It made a full pass down the street."

"Was it the same one?" she asked Chris. She offered Jack and Maggie a weak nod and tried to focus on her conversation.

"Yes, it was moving slowly, definitely checking out the Colter house. I think they saw me. I tried to follow the truck but lost it out on highway 64 close to Etowah. I'm beginning to think the threat to the Colters might just be real."

"I agree," Shelby concurred, feeling very uneasy. "Look, today I am going with Mrs. Colter's son; he is taking me on a drive on the Blue Ridge Parkway. I'd appreciate it if you kept an eye on the ....ah...book the other book."

"What book?" Chris asked sounding puzzled. "Oh, you mean Maggie Colter."

"Yes, that one," Shelby quickly replied.

"Will do," Chris agreed, then added with a chuckle, "you know Shelby, Jack is considered quite a catch around here."

"Oh hush up," she hissed into the phone. "I'm not going to argue with you about this any more. Now, have a good day. I'll talk to you later."

With a weak smile, she shook her head at Maggie and Jack and slipped the phone back into its carrying case. With a sigh, she professed, "Agents!"

"Well, it's going to be a beautiful day for a drive on the Parkway," Maggie said, rising from the table with her coffee cup.

Jack seemed amused. To Shelby's great annoyance he hadn't stopped smiling at her since she walked into the room. Why did he have to be so darn good-looking?

Maggie picked up the coffee pot and refilled their cups. "Well, it's certainly a beautiful day. I know the two of you are going to have a wonderful time on the Parkway."

"Why don't you come with us?" Shelby suggested, trying to keep her voice even. Maggie's presence would certainly hinder any more intimate moments.

Maggie shook her head, "Oh no, you kids run along. I'm sure Jack will be an excellent guide. Behave yourself, young man."

"Of course," Jack promised with a polite chuckle.

She hid behind a sip of coffee. Maggie's lie was beginning to haunt her, she thought, looking out into the garden. And, she wondered how many more lies would she have to tell Jack this day?

"I already have a cooler packed with ice, soft drinks, and water," Jack said, coming to his feet. "I thought we would have lunch on the Parkway. There is a beautiful little hotel and restaurant with a nice overlook atop Pisgah Mountain."

"That is a wonderful idea, Jack. Silver will enjoy the Pisgah Inn." Maggie concurred, "You two run along now."

With Jack's eyes wide, excited, and impatient upon her, she had little to do but go upstairs and gather her things. Her things included a small 9 millimeter glock handgun which she placed into her holster purse.

The purse was specially designed with a compartment to conceal a gun. It was separate from the car keys and makeup. She slipped the Velcro strap over the handgun. The purse's extra padding reinforced the hold and discreetly concealed her handgun. Though she had a special permit which allowed her to carry a concealed weapon, today, she was more concerned about concealing her 'secret identity'.

For good measure, she picked up the camera and small notebook she had remembered to pack in her suitcase the day before. Jack would expect her to have these things. She knew she would have to play her part well to get through the day.

Shelby heard a light tap on her door. Turning, Shelby saw Maggie and motioned for her to come in the room.

"I was wondering," Maggie began, "was that phone call anything to do with Jack?"

"I'm not sure," Shelby replied, measuring each word, "at least nothing we can be sure about at the moment. We are continuing to chase a few leads down today. We may have something later."

"We?" Maggie asked.

Shelby closed her purse. "When I need more man hours than I can handle, I hire my former partner, Chris Turner, who still works at the Hendersonville Police Department. I trust him with my life and I most certainly trust him with your son's life."

Maggie nodded. "I'm not worried about that. If he works for you, I'm sure he is trustworthy. You just go off and enjoy the day with Jack and don't worry about a thing."

"It's my job to worry, Maggie, and to keep your son safe," Maggie replied, wondering who was going to keep her safe from Jack.

"From everything I have seen so far," Maggie said, her eyes shining bright, "I think everything is turning out better than even I planned."

Shelby stopped and looked straight at Maggie, "What do you mean 'turning out better than you had planned?'"

Maggie's eyes flashed then widened, but she was not caught off guard, "Why that you are here, and my son is safe. What else could I possibly mean?"

Indeed, Shelby thought.

"Maggie," Shelby said in a whisper, "are you hiding something from me?"

"Me? Oh no," came Maggie's too quick response. Shelby knew she was lying.

Maggie smiled sweetly. "Run along dear, have a nice day."

Shelby stared at Maggie. Her innocent demeanor was fooling no one, especially her. Shelby shook her head and followed her heart down to the first floor.

"Ready?" Jack called from the front door. He escorted her out to the Ford Bronco and opened the passenger side door.

Slipping into the seat, Jack brought down the safety belt around her waist and snapped it into place. He took a moment to make sure it was both comfortable and secure. "Just part of the service," he said with a grin.

Shelby gave him a soft smile. Didn't he know the mere touch of his fingertips on her skin caused an unexpected flutter in the pit of her stomach? She decided she wouldn't tell him.

Maggie had walked out on the porch and waved goodbye.

"Ready?" Jack asked in a low, silver voice.

Shelby laughed. "I was born ready."

Jack chuckled and scanned her form with critical approval. Unexpectedly her heart skipped a pace. It was just too easy to get lost in the way he looked at her. She tried to slow her pulse to a more even beat, but her heart fluttered erratically. His attraction to her was both flattering and magnetic. She felt like a moth unable to alter its path toward a light. His eyes were disarming, his nearness unsettling. Decidedly, she would have to look elsewhere for distraction this day.

As the Ford Bronco began to weave through the streets, Jack began to point out area landmarks.

"You might find it interesting to note that Hendersonville was once the favorite hunting grounds of the Cherokee. Since the 1920s, however, it's been a summer resort town, though you will find some argument there with our local folks who enjoy mild winters here. Hendersonville is host to the North Carolina Apple Festival and several annual events. As far as cities go, we have an art center, and a symphony orchestra. We also play host to the North Carolina State Theater at East Flat Rock."

Jack's voice was pleasant, rich in sultry tones that resonated though her body. She had only to listen and occasionally nod to his narrate. While the words may not hold her interest, the man certainly did, and today there was no escaping him.

Not quite midmorning, the traffic was light. The morning air was cool and her whole body was unnerved with his nearness. Carolina pines and 100 year old oaks that lined the buildings and offices of Hendersonville gave way to impressive main gates of some of the area's most exclusive neighborhoods at the outskirts of town. Gradually the vistas changed once again from rolling hillside golf communities to stately farm houses that sat against the dramatic backdrop of low-lying mountains.

Outside Etowah, the road curved just a bit. Nearing the Holmes State Forest turn off, Shelby happened to glance at the Gas and Go Convenience Store located at the turn off. She bolted upright. A brown pick up truck was at the gas pump.

Grasping for an excuse to stop, she stammered, "Would you mind stopping? I need more film for my camera."

"Sure," Jack replied.

He drove the Bronco into the Gas and Go parking lot. Jack appeared to be very much enjoying the day.

Whether she surprised him or not, Shelby jumped out of the vehicle and hurried toward the store. Nearing the Ford truck, she slowed her pace keeping her full attention on the two men who had emerged from the truck.

Shelby took note of the license plate. She was sure it was the same number Chris had given to her. She glanced back at Jack. He was occupied with his radio.

She turned her attention back to the poorly dressed men at the pump. The men were arguing as to who was going to pay for the gas. Apparently the younger of the two lost the argument. With unkempt hair down over his forehead, he passed right in front of her. Shelby quickly noted his height, his weight, hair color, clothing, and the type of shoes he wore. She scanned for jewelry, tattoos, and details.

Inside the store, she grabbed 35 mm film at the counter display and stood directly behind the man who was busy counting out a few dollar bills. He mumbled something to the clerk and was out the door as quickly as he had entered.

Shelby again watched both men and kept a guarded eye on Jack.

The argument resumed when the young man returned to the truck. Shelby stuck the film in her pocket and made ready to take their picture. If noticed by either, she would appear just another tourist photographing the mountain ridge behind them.

Noticing her, Jack stepped out of the Bronco and came toward her.

"Step over here," Shelby urged him. "I'll take your picture."

"Sure," Jack said, sounding pleased and flattered at her request.

Not only was Jack facing away from the men, but she had a clear view of both of them and the truck.

Jack, a veteran of numerous catalog photo shoots, put his hands on his hips and gave her a sharp profile. Snap, she took a picture of Jack with the camera's focus on the men and the truck behind him. Snap, snap. Jack began to playfully pose for her.

He flexed his biceps, chuckling to himself, and then brought his massive arms in front of him to give her full dimension of his physique. Shelby smiled weakly, wishing he would step out of the shot.

"This is my best superman pose," Jack called out to her with laughter and placed his hands squarely on his hips. He turned his head giving her a side profile of his handsome face.

Shelby snapped the camera; certain she got the corner of Jack's nose and a clean shot of the younger man.

She side-stepped Jack to get a better picture of the older man, but Jack matched her movements blocking the shot.

Paying no attention to either Shelby or Jack, the men jumped into the truck. It roared to life.

Snap, snap, she now had the side views of the truck and a clear shot of the license plate as the old truck pulled out of the station.

Turning back to Jack, she was surprised to find him still preening in a ridiculous pose.

"Where does that road go?" She called out to him, eager to follow the men.

Rushing back to the Bronco, she ignored Jack's look of disappointment. Ego maniac, she thought with a chuckle, jumping into the vehicle.

If he had been disappointed, it was forgotten by the time he slipped behind the steering wheel. "That road leads to Holmes Educational Forest. As a matter of fact, you may be interested in..."

"Great!" Shelby cried before he finished, "let's go!"

Jack looked perplexed but not unpleasant. He turned the key and the engine roared to life.

"Hurry," Shelby urged him. There was no logical explanation for her abrupt behavior except the truth. Instead, she lied, "I've read about Holmes Educational Forest. It would be great for my book."

"Well, then," Jack said, his good nature restored, "if you want to go there, I will take you post haste."

Oh please, Shelby cried inside, hurry.

Jack turned the key in the ignition switch and the Bronco roared to life.

He smiled to himself. First the grand dinner last night, and then taking his photos. He couldn't remember when a woman showed so much interest in him. This pleased him more than he wanted to admit. He coughed nervously and with a smile said, "I'm very flattered that you wanted to take my picture."

"Yes!" Shelby said, trying not to sound annoyed, "you're welcome. Listen, could we please hurry!"

Jack took precious seconds in pulling out of the parking space.

Hurry, hurry, hurry, she was screaming inside, but gave Jack a weak smile.

The Ford truck had been moving slowly and Jack's Bronco easily overtook them.

Ahead of them, the truck slowed, pulling up behind a county maintenance tractor. Mowing the grassy shoulder of the road, it had slowed the traffic following it. Luck, she thought resting back in the seat, was on her side.

It was at that exact moment that the truck pulled past the slow moving county mowing tractor and vanished from her view.

Stay calm. Shelby told herself, trying to quail her anxiety. The truck had been traveling at a slow pace, she reminded herself, they would be upon them soon enough.

However, as Jack and Shelby neared the maintenance vehicle, it jolted to a complete halt. Shelby almost screamed out loud as the Bronco slowed to a full stop. She waited impatiently for the county road tractor to complete the left turn.

Shelby was barely aware of her own fingernails sinking deep into the palm of her hand. Struggling to maintain a calm demeanor, she waited impatiently for oncoming traffic to pass.

"Just five more miles," Jack said, reading her anxiety for the wrong reasons. She had lost the ability to speak.

At last the tractor turned down the dirt farm road. Ahead of them the two lane highway was free of traffic. The truck had vanished.

"Damn," Shelby said under her breath. They had lost the men and the truck.

Disappointed, she leaned back against the seat and pattered her camera. She drew some small measure of consolation from the photos she had taken. The truck was gone. Still, she thought raising slightly in her seat, perhaps she could find it parked in front of one of the old frame houses that lined the road.

Turning to Jack, she offered him an appreciative smile. She protectively traced the outline of the handgun in her purse.

On either side of them sleek horses grazed in thick green pastures. Passing a farmhouse she saw two children were riding tricycles and a third was swinging in an old tire swing. From the back porch, their mother called out to the children as she shook out a kitchen rug.

The day seemed so ordinary. Nothing was out of place. Nothing was unusual. And yet, Shelby thought looking down the road, somewhere in the in the serene tranquility of a common day lay a very real and present danger.

CHAPTER FIVE

In the distance Shelby could see the majestic Blue Ridge Mountains. Though miles away, they loomed large and imposing, dominating the landscape with their exquisite beauty. Low-lying clouds hung over the mountain chain obscuring the long craggy ridge that stretched on for more miles than the eye could see.

Gradually the mountains became lost in tall trees that lined either side of the two lane highway. Closer still, multicolored patches of wildflowers covered the roadside, occasionally spilling over pavement along the shoulder.

The truck had disappeared.

With a sigh of resignation, Shelby realized the truck was either safely hidden behind a house or perhaps had turned onto a country road. Either way, there was no trace of it or the men. They had vanished into thin air. They had seemingly vanished into thin air. Shelby leaned against the seat and patted the camera. She had at least managed to take a picture of the truck and more importantly, she had a picture of the license.

Absorbed in her own thoughts, she was startled when Jack turned from the main road onto the gravel entrance of Holmes Regional Forest.

With an irresistibly devastating grin, Jack turned to her and said, "You'll enjoy this."

Shelby couldn't help but return his infectious smile and tried to concentrate on her surroundings. After all, she reminded herself, she was a tourist, or at least pretending to be one. This was an assignment, not a date. She tried to focus her attention wholly on the short tree-lined drive and not the man beside her. Less than a quarter mile away into the State Park, the road opened into a grassy parking lot.

Though only one of six educational forests in North Carolina, this beautiful State Park offered visitors a living environmental education center. Local hikers and residents took full advantage of the trails, grassy knolls, and rustic picnic areas nestled among the trees; for the most part it was bypassed by tourists who failed to realize the treasures Holmes Forest offered.

Jack brought the Bronco to a full stop. Shelby opened her car door without waiting for him to come to her side.

A look of disappointment swept across his face as apparently he wanted to play the gentleman. Shelby looked down at the rocky soil beneath her feet, the less she made this feel like a date, the better for both of them.

When she looked back up, she noticed Jack retrieving two designer water bottles from a large cooler.

"You'll need this," he said, offering her one of the bottles.

She managed a small smile and accepted the water. As she accepted the water, their fingers touched. The seemingly casual touch spread from her fingertips down her arm in a warm blaze of unmistakable exhilaration that left butterflies in her stomach. Swallowing hard, she tried to remain calm and once again reminded herself she was on assignment.

Their eyes met and a strange soft light radiated, filled his eyes with wonder. For a moment, he seemed taken back but then rallied quickly. Clearing his throat, he said, "Let's do some sightseeing."

"Sure," Shelby agreed, looking in the direction of the forest path. Taking uneven steps, she tried to tell herself the moment had been nothing at all and yet it had been everything that could never be spoken or even dreamed about. She took a firm grip on the bottle and reminded herself she couldn't afford to be distracted by silly notions. Besides, she told herself, with a well-practiced line, today he'd be nice, tomorrow he'll be breaking her heart with his lies. Jack's not like that, a small voice argued. Her stomach took an unexpected twist and she hurried toward a small wooden bridge and away from her heart.

A small creek trickled between the parking lot and the park and she hurried across it to where a large glass display case offered visitors a map showing trail heads and information about the Talking Trees.

Though Shelby had lived in Hendersonville for years she had only been to Holmes Forest on two occasions. One of her clients renewed their vows under the rustic wood pavilion here, and second was the Henderson County Law Enforcement outing. On both occasions, she had stayed in the picnic area not venturing into the park itself.

Jack busied himself reading the display information about the cost and damages of forest fires, the importance of a managed forest, and good forest management.

Shelby took a moment, looking about quickly get her bearings. The path to their left led to the restroom and facilities, the trail to the right to the picnic areas. The main path between the two led to the Talking Trees, the hiking trails, and educational areas. Satisfied, she turned her attention to the various hiking trails.

"Okay, I give up, what exactly are the Talking Trees?"

Jack laughed and tenderly reached down and covered her small hand in his larger one. His expression was flirtatious and he was clearly taking charge of the moment. Struggling to remain calm, she tried to think of a logical reason to simply slip her hand from his but could think of no polite way to do this. Besides, she didn't want to. She knew how to handle a man who was a liar and a cheat. Jack Colter was neither.

"Come on," he said playfully with a laugh that was rich and pleasant. She decided she liked the sound of it.

The path they were walking on was bordered by a thick mixture of mountain hardwood, rhododendron, majestic oaks, towering birch trees, and black gum.

On the shady side of this mountain, the air was sweet to breathe in and cool to her senses. Only the quiet sounds of their hiking boots chewing the small pebbles and leaves on the forest floor. The beauty of God's handiwork was surreal and made small work of any human worries or cares.

Walking up the steep incline, Jack held Shelby's hand just a bit tighter. "I should get away from the store more. It seems a long time since I've actually enjoyed my life."

Despite herself, Shelby laughed. "Yes, I know the feeling."

"Well, to be honest, I just haven't met anyone I wanted to spend what little time I had with." He stopped and added, "Until now. I like you Silver, you're a very interesting lady."

"I suppose I should say thank you," Shelby said, keeping her voice soft. She held her gaze steady, not happy with this turn in the conversation. "I've heard most men want a woman like their mothers."

Jack howled with laughter causing a flutter of wings in a nearby bush. "Not me! I love my mother and would be happy to expound on her virtues, she's the most conniving woman you could ever meet, in a nice way, of course, but trust me; you have no idea what she is capable of."

It was Shelby's turn to laugh. With a toss of her head she replied in a cool tone, "Oh yes I do!"

Jack stopped abruptly and pointed to an opening in the trail. "Look, the paw print of a black bear. Don't be afraid."

"I'm not," she said patting the gun in her carry purse.

"Bear once ruled these mountains," Jack said, looking at the imprint. "Now there's just over 2000 in all of the Western Carolina Mountains. But, like I said, don't be afraid, they don't want to see us any more than we want to walk unexpectedly up to them."

"Have you ever come upon one?"

"Several times, while they are beautiful to look at, they are not domesticated animals. People forget and try to feed them, take pictures with them. These are wild animals and that sort of activity will only result in serious danger."

Jack's expression grew serious. He paused a moment before he continued. "Black bears like most wild animals are losing their habitat to man. We're destroying their food sources, their water and their homes. As a company we have work with several environmental groups, and of course, the Boy Scouts."

"Were you in the Boy Scouts?" Shelby asked, already suspecting the answer.

"Yes, I was, and I became an Eagle Scout as a matter of fact. My dad was the scoutmaster and I can't tell you what a magical childhood I had growing up here in these mountains. Someday, I'd like to have my son..." Jack's voice broke suddenly, and when he spoke again there was a slight tremor in his voice, as though he had struck a cord deep within his soul. "Well, someday I'd like to have a son and teach him the values, and have the adventures my dad had with me. Good grief, did I just embarrass myself? Sorry Silver, I guess I'm a mile away from the men in your world."

Listening to Jack speak, she had gotten lost in his words and lowered her gaze to hide the thoughts and feelings that were assaulting her.

"You're right," she said softly, "you're unlike any man in my world, but take that as a good thing. And Jack, wanting to be a good father is certainly something every man should want for himself. Thank you for sharing that with me."

Changing the subject, she took the lead and pulled him away from the paw print and the loneliness they both felt. "So if I'm attacked by a bear, what should I do?"

"If you're attacked by any other bear," Jack began, "you should cover your head and play dead. The average bear will lose interest and walk away. Despite being the smallest of the American bears, black bears are the most dangerous. Silver, if a black bear ever attacks, you will need to fight back. But, you needn't worry, just stay close to me."

Shelby frowned. She knew full well that any black bear who had wandered though over night was long gone.

"Ah, the *Talking Trees*," Jack said as the larger trail narrowed to a smaller walkway. "This will be the first of, I think, of seven."

Winding their way up the path, they stopped in front of a giant poplar. Jack reached over to a small kiosk and pressed a small red button.

The cheerful strands of bluegrass music filled the air from its prerecorded box. Above the music a male voice said, "Hi, I'm a poplar tree. I grow over 150 feet tall."

"I see, *The Talking Trees*," Shelby said with a smile, and the message continued to tell more about the poplar. "This is cute. I can see why children would love to come here."

Jack seemed pleased to have pleased her.

Midmorning, there were no hikers or heavy travel, in fact they had the beautiful half mile stroll through the talking trees to themselves.

Listening to Jack speak about the forest or point out a flower or the squirrel that had come to watch them, Shelby felt her entire body relax. So lost in the deep green of the woods, and the pleasant sound of his voice, the trees, Shelby felt the stresses and momentarily confusion of her life slip away, leaving her with a sense of peace and tranquility. Somewhere in the deep greens of the forest trail, she made the decision to simply enjoy the day. Why not? She was after all doing the job she was assigned to do; there was no harm in taking a small bit of pleasure for herself.

With a sense of peace she hadn't felt in a long time, they traveled along the easy trail going from one *Talking Tree* to the next. Despite the places where the trail narrowed and then opened into the woods, Jack never once let go of her hand.

They reached the parking lot just in time to see two Henderson County school buses pull into the lot. Children filled every window and their laughter resonated with excitement.

They both smiled as the kids began pouring off the bus, eager for the field trip away from school.

Jack walked with her to the passenger side of his Bronco and unlocked the door for her.

"Thank you," Shelby said, slipping into the seat. "That was very nice."

Jack carefully closed the door, walked about the vehicle, and sat behind the wheel.

"If you are not too hungry," he said inserting the key into the ignition, "I'd like to drive you to the Blue Ridge Parkway.

We can grab a bite at the Pisgah Inn. It's a restaurant that sits atop the Parkway with some really spectacular views."

"Jack, for the first time in a long time, I'm in no hurry whatsoever. That sounds nice."

Leaving Holmes Educational Forest, Shelby made a promise to revisit the State Park. Struggling to hold onto the magic she had felt just moments ago proved hopeless as they left the park. Looking out the window, she realized Jack and his laugh, his easy comfortable presence, would forever haunt this place in her mind. A whimsical part of her wished all was at it seemed and that she was Silver Lake, not a private investigator.

As they pulled back onto the highway, Jack began to tell her more about Henderson County and Hendersonville's history. She knew he was trying hard to be a good host and listening to him speak; she could freely take in his handsome features, his lips, and his deep blue eyes. She was conscious of his every move, his even breath. She was already beginning to miss him and he hadn't even left.

He finished with a Cherokee Indian tale and began pointing out some landmarks and stories of his life growing up in the mountains.

Shelby remembered to keep an eye out for the Ford truck, but it was

no where to be found. She had nothing to do but enjoy the day.

Almost at the entrance to Pisgah Forest, they stopped at a red light. Without thinking she turned to look out the window, and to her horror saw a friend, Don Russell from the Brevard Police Department. Off duty and in his own vehicle, he smiled and waved at Shelby before motioning her to roll down the window.

For Jack's sake, she tried to manage a look of confusion as if she didn't recognize the universal signal for rolling down one's window.

Jack had noticed. The frown on his face was dark and menacing.

Shelby turned back to her off-duty friend who was once again gesturing her to speak to him. Her stomach lurched. She felt she had little choice but to roll down the window. God, if you're not too busy laughing at me, she prayed fervently, please, please, make this darn light turn green.

The light suddenly turned green and the car behind Jack gave him an angry honk for not pulling forward.

Hallelujah, her heart sang hallelujah, hallelujah, hal-le-lu-jah! She waved a goodbye to her friend and made a note to give him a call later.

"Everyone is so friendly here," she said leaning back into the passenger seat, trying to avoid looking at Jack who was clearly annoyed.

"Yeah," Jack said, his voice in a near growl.

Shelby would have liked to have told Jack that Don Russell was an old friend, happily married with two grown daughters and childsons. She sat feeling curiously amused; her delight was in perfect and equal proportion to Jack's irritability.

Looking out the window trying to concentrate on the beautiful mountain scenery, she filled with irony. She had always prided herself with her ability to remain cool and aloof by circumstances. Yet, sitting next to him, she found herself hanging on his words. Her heart was pounding and taking her places she could never go with Jack Colter. The moment he realized she was fostering a lie, this little make believe world would vanish in the smokey hues of the Blue Ridge Mountains.

Guard yourself, Shelby MacGregor, she warned herself fearing her entanglement with Jack Colter was growing by the moment.

Why couldn't she just tell him, she thought, then looked and saw his dazzling smile. Then she remembered her promise to Maggie Colter.

Just a few more hours she thought, then this ruse will be over; she could be Shelby MacGregor and leave the lie of Silver Lake behind her. For now, she must keep her false identity and any fanciful sentiment and notions to herself. Good grief, she concluded, maybe I am cut out to be a romance writer, and she certainly was developing the imagination for it!

Driving through the main entrance of Pisgah, her senses, her fears, and her temporary new career were forgotten in the deep, dark, rich, green of the forest.

Midsummer the leafy trees were in full foliage. Treetops reached high toward the Carolina blue sky. Though not quite noon, long cool shadows stretched across the roadway. The forest presented visitors with an astonishing contrast of brilliant sunlight and lush tender shade. In places, branches and limbs crossed over the road creating a natural canopy over the timberline. Lush green grasses added to the scenery filling the human senses with tranquility and soothing calm.

The Davidson River ran alongside the road and its melodious sound of rushing water over a rocky riverbed filled the air with a pleasant euphoric mood of tranquility. Bright yellow and white sparkles of sunlight danced across the shallow river. Nothing could make this day more complete, Shelby thought in peaceful silence.

"Let's stop here," Jack said, pulling into the ranger station.

Shelby bolted upright. Well, at least nothing but stopping in this busy parking lot. Alert, she scanned the immediate area. Most vehicles were out of state. This did not to pacify her.

Exposure at this moment would not be a pretty sight.

As usual the ranger station was busy with out-of-towners looking at several displays of mountain trout and wildlife of the area. The small gift shop was crowded with tourists examining books, knickknacks, and souvenirs of the Pisgah Forest.

Relieved to find no one she knew, she decided she'd best act the part of a quintessential tourist this day.

Jack duly followed her around, but drifted away from her toward the book section.

Despite her best intention, she saw him reading one of her favorite books on hiking. She came up to him and said, "I bet I've read that book a dozen times! The trails are unbelievable, wonderful."

Jack closed the book and glanced at the cover.

"Really?" he asked, his voice filled with curiosity. He looked back at the cover and read, *"Little Known Hiking Trails Along the Blue Ridge."*

Too late she realized her error. Nervously she bit her lip and felt her body shudder. She felt impaled by the questioning look in his eyes.

"You have hiked these trails?"

"Ah, I'm ah," Shelby stammered, feeling the scream of frustration at the back of her throat. How could she have been so stupid? She decided to deftly cover her tracks.

"Did I say I hiked those trails?" she said with a nervous laugh, "I meant I wanted, wanted to hike them. They seem so wonderful; the writer really did a good job. Makes you feel like you are really there!"

Before he had a chance to respond, she ducked away quickly grabbing an oversized stuffed plush black bear, coffee cup, and some postcards. She quickly added two books on the area for good measure and headed for the cashier.

"Your total is $ 43.50," the cashier said, carefully placing the bear into a gift bag.

Before Shelby had a time to pull out her wallet to pay for the purchase, Jack laid a gold Master Card on the counter. "This is on me."

Shelby started to protest but decided to accept the gift. She would repay him later.

On the way out of the door, for good measure, Shelby took a moment to grab every single brochure available and slipped them into her bag.

"There is a short half mile walk around the ranger station if you care to go there," Jack offered. The look on his face told her he was still contemplating her ill- timed comment and nervous rebuttal.

"I'm eager to see the Parkway," Shelby said, and hurried toward the Bronco.

When they got into the vehicle, Jack pulled the bear out and sat him upright in the back seat. Very cute. Shelby looked over her shoulder once to find the bear ginning at her, his little black lifeless eyes mocking her. She decided to ignore him too.

Leaving the ranger station minutes later, Jack leaned back against his seat. Her comment seemed forgotten, at least for the moment. She sent another prayer of thanks skyward and realized she had a definite skill at lying.

Taking the soft turns of the base of the mountain, she gradually began to relax once more and enjoy the day.

"We have to stop here," Jack said rounding a turn. He pulled behind several stopped cars along the roadway. Shelby heard the sound of Looking Glass Falls before she left the Bronco.

Walking along the walkway to the Falls, Jack's hard hand reached down and gently captured her hand into his. His touch seemed urgent and Shelby's heartbeat pounded in perfect rhythm with the sound of rushing waters. A hot ache burned in the back of her throat. Despite her apprehensions, her knees were weakening by the touch of his hand..

When they reached the top of the steps, they began a slow descent down the rock hued steps. The full view of the water plunging down a rock was immediately visible as it fell into a tranquil pool below. A thick vapor mist rose from the pool. Whatever was lost in height was captured in the sheer power and excitement of rushing water.

A safe distance from the waterfall, children and adults were climbing about the large boulders stopping occasionally to stare at the waterfall, as if completely memorized by the beauty.

Halfway down the steps, Jack stopped at a rustic overlook, and hesitating just a moment, his gaze was as soft as a caress as he searched her face for permission to touch her lips.

As their eyes met, Shelby was filled with a strange inner excitement, yes, yes, she wanted him to kiss her, more than life, she did want him to kiss her, even if only this once.

He didn't hesitate, sweeping her weightless into his arms. With the crashing sound of the waterfall in her ears, his lips feather-touched her with tantalizing pleasure. She drank in the sweetness, savoring the sweetness, her senses were reeling and she felt her body arch into his, giving over to a giddy sense of sweet surrender.

She felt drugged by his clean scent, the powerful grasp of his arms around her, and the succulent warmth of his kiss. Deep in an abyss of warming emotions, she heard a strange small voice calling out, urging her to resist the honeyed taste of his mouth, but her body and her soul refused.

Behind them thousands of gallons of water savagely poured over the cliff. It fell to the dark lagoon with such a force that it shook the ground beneath them. The fine mist rose from the fall moistening their skin, lightly dampening their hair, and filling their senses with an intoxicating blanket of sweet mountain air.

Though she had no right, she wanted to remember this moment and keep it safe in her heart. The sweetheart kiss stopped all too soon as Jack pulled reluctantly away from her.

"And I promised myself I would be a gentleman today," he said in a teasing tone. A grin overtook his handsome features and he had yet to let her go.

Her lips were still on fire from his kiss as she said softly, "Gentlemen are sometimes highly overrated."

"You know, seems like I remember there's this old Cherokee legend that if you kiss a girl at the Looking Glass Falls, good luck will follow you the rest of your days."

Shelby laughed but made no effort to move away from him. "Really?"

"No," Jack said with a soft chuckle, "I just made it up."

Shelby laughed again. She felt her full lips curl into a soft smile. She knew at this moment she would forgive this man anything, but would he forgive her when he found out the truth?

"Come on, let's go down and splash around the falls."

Eager to follow him anyway, Shelby allowed herself to be led to the boulders around the base of the waterfall.

"You're very beautiful," Jack called out over the roar of water. His voice was smooth and velvet edged and evoked a strange feeling of euphoria within her. How, at this moment, she longed to truly let herself go, but a lie stood between them. She bit her lip to keep from telling him the truth.

Two teens scampered around them and hurried too close to the falls. A woman, presumably their mother, called out to them but they either didn't or pretended not to hear. Reaching their destination, they stopped and seemed to almost race back along their same path, this time uttering a "sorry" as they passed Jack and Shelby.

Shelby and Jack remained at the Falls just a moment longer before retracing their steps back to the Bronco.

"I'm hungry," Jack said with a grin. "What say we go get some lunch? I know just the place, the Pisgah Inn."

Despite everything she knew was inherently wrong with this adventure, she couldn't help but feel lighthearted as they pulled back onto the main road taking them to the top of the mountain.

The road was filled with tourists who were winding their way along the scenic drive. No one was in a hurry; they were too busy enjoying the scenery.

Jack slowed the Bronco twice; first as a car full of teens pulled into Sliding Rock Park. Just beyond Sliding Rock, most of the cars ahead of them turned off into The Cradle of the Forestry, the Park's main visitor center. With a smile in Shelby's direction, Jack continued on.

Driving the winding curves toward the mountain's crest, they sat enjoying the ride and each other. No words were spoken; no words were necessary.

Shelby allowed the beauty and strength of the forest to fill her every sense. At this moment, she wanted nothing more, only to be at his side. It felt natural, safe, warm, and mostly it just felt right. What had begun as an ordinary day had turned into magic. She was afraid if she spoke, no matter how trivial the thought, the moment and the spell would be broken.

At the pentacle of the crest, the main road passed under a gray stone bridge. Jack took a right, easing the Bronco onto the Blue Ridge Parkway.

High along the crest, they could see deep blue mountain ranges stretching for miles upon miles in endless waves of plateaus and distant ridges.

Built in the 1930 as a Depression Era public works project, the Parkway stretched from Georgia to Virginia. Overlooks complete with ample parking and legends about each point offered a more dramatic and stunning vista than the one before. The Western North Carolina Mountains stretched long across the horizon in a never-ending panorama of natural wonder. Rich, lush foliage that stretched across the distant mountain like thick green carpet and above them high on the rim of the Blue Ridge there was unity between peace and sky.

A mile on the Parkway, they passed a small black and white skunk ambling peacefully along the roadway, oblivious to passers-by who had stopped to take his picture. Shelby smiled at the tourists who were intent on taking his photo for prosperity and friends back home. As if it was just too much an effort to lift his tail and leave an indelible impression for the annoying visitors, the little animal turned and looked at them once before disappearing into a thicket of rhododendron. Shelby knew small herds of deer and other forest animals were nearby but it was midday, and they were resting in cool, secluded hollows.

"Hope you are hungry," Jack said at the first sign of the Pisgah Inn.

"Yes, I am. " Shelby said with a smile and for good measure added, "Are we far from the Inn?"

"Yes, and in my mind, you aren't going to find a more beautiful restaurant in Western North Carolina."

Shelby listened with interest realizing she had never learned its history or how this quaint little hotel, restaurant, and gift store came to be on the Parkway. It simply sat a haven for tourists who needed gas, a chance to rest on top of the world, or an unbelievably delicious meal of fresh smoked fresh mountain trout. Like the Parkway itself, the Pisgah Inn was open only in the spring, summer, and fall. It was closed and inaccessible during thick winter snows that blanketed the region.

"As a local, I have to say I'm prejudiced, but I think when you see it you'll realize it commands one of the most picturesque views in the area. You'll see why in just a few minutes because it's actually 5,000 feet above sea level and its only open in spring, summer, and fall. Like the Parkway, it's closed during the winter, as the road is impassible with snow."

"Where did the name Pisgah come from?" Shelby asked, "I suppose it's an old Cherokee Indian name."

Jack laughed. "You'd think so, but as I recall the original name for Pisgah was Elseetoss and the natives called this ridge Warwasseeta. When General Rutherford came through here in 1776, a minister with the group renamed the area Mount Pisgah from the fourth chapter of Deuteronomy when Moses went up on the mountain and proclaimed the Promised Land to the Israelites."

"Seems appropriate," Shelby said as they pulled into the parking lot of the Pisgah Inn. "The view is absolutely breathtaking."

"Yes it is," Jack agreed, helping her out of the car. "You might be interested to know that in 1914, the Forestry Service purchased nearly 80,000 acres from Edith Vanderbilt and the Pisgah Inn opened in 1919."

"I had no idea," Shelby said as they made their way toward the restaurant. "Jack, you're a walking encyclopedia."

Jack laughed. "Actually, knowing I was going to be your tour guide today I took a few moments to refresh my memory about the history of the Inn."

Guilt washed over her again. Here he was treating her to what she would perceive as an extraordinary adventure and she was busy spying on him. Tormented by the gnawing knot that chewed at her insides, she took a deep sigh. The truth would be out soon enough and she'd best enjoy these few stolen hours with her handsome guide. Besides, in the end there would surely be no harm, permanent harm for her or for Jack.

Inside the Pisgah Inn, she wandered into the gift shop leaving Jack alone to study the menu just outside the restaurant's entrance.

Glistening metallic and copper wind chimes dangled from the ceiling and a CD of mountain music filled the room along with an exceptional array of unique handmade Appalachian crafts, t-shirts, and delectable homemade treats. The clerk waved a welcome to her but went back to helping a couple at the register sort through their postcards and souvenirs. A stunning pair of earrings caught her eye but she knew Jack was waiting in the lobby.

"Oh man," Jack said, "I thought I knew exactly what I wanted when I came in here, but looking at the menu I can't decide whether I'm going to have the fresh mountain trout or Pisgah Pasta."

Scanning through the lunchtime menu selection of salads, sandwiches, Shelby had a full view of the restaurant. Windows surrounded the dining room offering every guest a stunning vista while they enjoyed their meal.

In the far corner, something caught her eye. No, she screamed internally, not here, not now!

Seated in the far corner of the restaurant, Red Chandler was sitting at a table with a woman who was not his wife. Shelby knew this because she busted Red Chandler a little over a year ago for having an affair with his secretary.

She glared at Red. White fury was coursing through her veins and set every nerve in her body on fire. She could feel her fingers shake as she watched Red reach his hand across the table toward his buxom blonde companion. The woman seemed not to notice the wedding ring still on his left finger. At that moment she wasn't sure who she wanted to strangle first, Red, or the floozy who was knowingly having a romantic lunch with a married man.

Shelby remembered Red's long-suffering wife, who despite indisputable proof of her husband's infidelity had forgiven him.

Shelby almost jumped at the sound of Jack's warm voice.

"I think I'll go with the fresh trout after all," Jack said, turning to her. "Ready? I'm hungry and think I'll start with smoked trout appetizer. You're going to love it Silver, I guarantee."

Shelby was no longer hungry. She would have loved nothing better than to march over to Red's table and demand to be introduced to his "friend." Red Chandler's look of surprise, however delicious that moment would be, would hardly be worth her own exposure to Jack.

Fortunately, Red was so engrossed with the blonde, he scarcely noticed the waitress when she brought their salads.

Shelby glanced about it the dining room. Long after the lunch time hour, the restaurant was nearly empty. Surely Red would notice her if she and Jack were seated. Having first hand knowledge of Red's nasty confrontational scene a year earlier, she could only guess his reaction of seeing her now. With Jack close, she had no choice but to retreat, at least for the moment.

"Shall we?" Jack asked again. His warm offer melted into a sweet smile.

"Jack," Shelby said stammered, "it's just all so beautiful outside, I'd really love to have a picnic lunch. Could we just grab some sandwiches?"

If Jack was disappointed, he didn't show it. "Sure, if it pleases you, of course. As a matter of fact a picnic on the Parkway sounds like a great idea. If you go outside, there's a beautiful view from the observation deck. Why don't you wait for me there?"

Giving Red Chandler a last glance, she turned and headed out the door.

At the moment there was simply nothing she could do. Silently she set a date with Red. It's you and me buddy, old pal, she thought, savoring that future moment. She walked outside, leaving Jack to give their order to the hostess.

Walking out to the Pisgah Inn's observation deck, she pulled her cell phone from her pocket and called Chris.

"I think I saw the stolen truck this morning," she said to him, and quickly repeated the South Carolina license tag number.

"That's it," Chris said in a voice that was low and smooth. "Where?"

"At the gas station out on Highway 64 by Holmes Forest, and I'll explain later, but I also managed to get a few shots of the driver and a passenger. As soon as I get them developed, I'll get you copies."

"That's great Shelby, say where are you now? You are coming in loud and clear."

Shelby laughed. "I'm on top of Mount Pisgah. Jack is buying us a picnic lunch at the Pisgah Inn."

"That explains it," Chris said with a chuckle. "So how goes it? Enjoying the life of a romance novelist?"

"It's tough," Shelby answered without hesitation, "and I have yet to write my first word. Good grief, on top of everything else, we pulled up next to Don Russell, one of the Brevard police officers, just before we entered the Pisgah Forest and I just dodged Red Chandler and his latest at the Pisgah Inn."

Chris grunted. "Thought ole Red learned his lesson the last time. Jack still doesn't have a clue as to who you are?"

"Not yet," Shelby said, seeing Jack approach, "look, Chris, I have got to go, talk to you later."

She ended the call and stuck the phone back into her pants pocket.

"My agent," Shelby explained, again wondering how long she could keep using that excuse.

Jack nodded, "A picnic basket will be ready in about ten minutes. Say,

how about I take a picture of you?"

At that moment two young men in hiking gear walked out onto the wooden overlook.

Borrowing Shelby's camera, Jack tossed it to the taller of the two. "We're here on our honeymoon. Could I get you to take our photos?"

Shelby, the hiker, and his friend looked at each other and grinned. "Absolutely."

"Pretty girl," the young man said, focusing the camera on Shelby. Jack snuggled closer to her and gave her a wink as they waited for the hiker to take their picture.

With an appreciative glance at Shelby, the hiker took the shot and with an all too knowing smile returned the camera to Jack. Shelby felt an unwelcome blush burn her cheeks. The moment the two men were out of sight, she turned to Jack and said, "Our honeymoon?"

"Someday," Jack said with an easy grin, "that is if you're lucky."

The heavy lashes that shadowed her cheeks flew up and in spite of herself she laughed. "If I'm lucky? Is that what you said, if I am lucky?"

Jack chuckled and managed to look sheepish. "All right, I meant if I'm lucky."

He grinned wickedly, and right on cue a young waitress brought out two large plastic bags to the observation deck. Jack gave her a generous tip as he took the bags from her.

With a glance at their order, Shelby looked at Jack. "Are we having company?"

"I told you I was hungry," he half apologized. "Let's find a picnic area Silver, and I think I know just the spot."

Some ten minutes later they pulled into an overlook area filled with empty picnic tables and a magnificent view of the valley below.

Allowing Shelby to choose a table, Jack began opening the bags. First came a small bottle of white wine, he set two plastic glasses before he began laying out several containers of food.

"Good grief Jack, did you order everything on the menu?"

Offering her a glass of white wine, he said, "Pretty much."

Shelby couldn't help but laugh and raised her glass to join him. "What exactly are we toasting?"

"To this perfect day," Jack announced, dramatically swinging his glass heavenward.

"I will drink to that," Shelby said in a voice pleased to join him in the toast. It was a perfect day.

With the touch of glasses, Jack's expression grew soft and he looked solemnly at Shelby. Her heart thundered erratically and she swallowed hard. He was attracted to her; a blind man could have seen that. And, she was helpless to stop her attraction to him; for every time she looked into his blue eyes, her heart turned in response and reminded her she was living a lie.

Watching him fill their plates with sandwiches and salads, Shelby was both flattered and ashamed of his interest in her. Though she had told herself time and time again this day to enjoy the moment; her composure was under attack. She had made it her life's mission not to trust men, not to fall in love, not to fall for a handsome face, and yet here she was with a man she was finding hard to resist.

Trying to concentrate on the lavish sandwich buffet he had set before her, she felt guilty. Her hands were trembling as she accepted the plate he offered and she wasn't sure if she could swallow.

"This is a perfect day," she managed, settling down in her seat.

For a stilled moment, Jack looked long at her. His blue eyes clouded with tenderness. "I think you would make any day perfect."

Stuffing her mouth full with chicken salad, Shelby felt her face burn and could think of no reply.

During the meal, Jack offered her more but she shook her head each time. Jack was quite content to tell her camping experiences he had had with his parents and with the Scouts when he was a boy. Shelby for her part was grateful just to listen without concocting more lies to add to her subterfuge.

With the meal complete, Shelby helped Jack dispose of the containers.

"So what do you think? Should I give up my day job and concentrate on showing these mountains to beautiful romance novelists?"

Shelby laughed. "Well, you are certainly doing a great job with me. Yes, I do believe you should consider it."

"You should know, Silver," he said softly, "that today is the first time in a very long time that I'm finally able to open up to someone, someone very special."

Shelby's heart jumped within her. She felt her body stiffen and the blood began to pound in her temples. She couldn't keep this lie between them one second more.

"Oh Jack," she said, ready to confess. "There's something I have to tell you! I have to tell you."

"Not now," he said, raising his hand to her to stop. "Look, I know there's something you are keeping from me. I know you want to tell me, feel you need to tell me, I have seen it more than once in your eyes. But right now, I don't want to hear anything that would spoil this day."

She bowed her head unsure of what to say or do.

"Good things take time, honey," he said, reaching out for her hand, "it takes time to get over old hurts and memories of the past. Whatever it is that is troubling you, don't worry.

Let's just enjoy the day, each other, and let tomorrow take care of itself."

With that, he rose and took her hand bringing it to his lips. "Not to worry sweetheart. Life has a way of working things out."

With her hand in his, Shelby stood feeling sad and exhausted. He obviously thought she was harboring some old hurt, and in part she was, but what would his reaction be when he found out everything about her was a lie?

CHAPTER SIX

J ack reached out for her hand. "Silver, honey, is it something
I said? You're trembling."

"Am I?" Shelby asked, looking down at her hands.

Jack's eyes filled with soft concern and his brow wrinkled
with tenderness.

Hesitant, she smiled. Maybe he was right. This wasn't
the right time to tell him the truth, perhaps she should keep
her secret until a time when she was better prepared, maybe
then he would be more accepting of her secret. Besides, Maggie
should be present for the big announcement. She decided to
confront Maggie when they returned. The truth had to come
out. In the meantime, she had to dissuade him with another
lie. "What's that old wives' saying? Someone walked across my
grave. Something like that."

"Are you being visited by old ghosts, honey?"

Shelby looked down at the ground then across to the
beautiful vista. The lines between fact and fiction were blurred.
She no longer trusted herself with Maggie's ruse even if it was
meant for Jack's safety.

What was the truth, she asked herself, and why couldn't
she just tell him in plain English? Whatever she was feeling,
she had to resist it. Her senses were reeling with years of hiding
emotions and denying feelings so private and aching she had
kept them at bay even from her heart. The pain of past, the
fleeting happiness of the present, and the fear of the future

whirled inside her threatening to fracture her heart into pieces. The turmoil was overwhelming. She had to be fair to Jack. She had to be fair to her client. She had to be fair to herself.

Her world needed to stop spinning. Looking at the long blue mountain range, Shelby knew she would at least stay true to herself. She had vowed not to hurt Jack. That was one promise she meant to keep.

Any need for confession would just have to wait until she spoke to Maggie. This was not the right time to offer confessions.

"Silver, you can talk to me about anything, anytime," Jack said, softly pulling her to him. "I don't know what is on your mind but whatever it is; I think if we give ourselves time, we just might be able to figure things out."

Shelby gave Jack a soft smile and hoped he would understand. She hoped he would understand about everything.

"I'm sorting out a lot of things," she stammered, trying to avoid yet another exquisite new lie. "Right now, I just need you to trust me."

His eyes were soft, filled with understanding. "I trust you, Silver."

She flinched as he said the name 'Silver' and she looked away before he saw more in her lying eyes.

Jack reached down and squeezed her hand. His eyes were once again filled with blanket trust and understanding.

For a brief moment, Shelby felt cheered. Maybe things would work out, could work out. She returned his soft smile and from a troubled heart said in a whisper, "Okay."

Back in the Bronco, they continued the drive along the Parkway. The scenery every bit as beautiful, the sweet scent of mountain air as fragrant as the morning, but somehow the magic of the morning had gone. Shelby knew it. Jack knew it. She could see Jack wanting to reconnect with her, but the lie stood between them. It was no longer Maggie's lie; it was hers.

Driving north toward Asheville, they left the high mountains turning off the Parkway to Highway 191 and followed the French Broad River toward Hendersonville. Jack once again assumed the role of guide and told her a bit more history of the area. Shelby half listened as she struggled with her conscience.

Nearing Hendersonville and the Colter house, Shelby rose up in her seat and smiled prettily at Jack.

"I'd really like these photos developed today. Would you mind stopping at the Eckerd's at the corner?" Shelby asked, her mind returning to the men in the photos. "I seem to recall they have a one-hour special."

"Of course," Jack said, all too happy to oblige her once again. "I'll wait in the car for you."

Thanking God for small favors, she practically fell out of the Bronco and hurried into the super drug store.

Kathy Mosley had been standing by the open window and seemed to note that Shelby was with Jack Colter. Her stoic expression never wavered when Shelby handed her two rolls of film.

"Hey, Shelby, how's it going?" Kathy greeted her.

"Just great," Shelby replied, with a glace out the window. Jack waved at her. Shelby turned nervously at Kathy. I really need these photos right away. Is there anyway you could..."

Kathy looked at the roll, her watch, and the other packages of film ahead of her. Looking at Kathy's eyes, Shelby knew Kathy was practically salivating to see what secrets were on the film, especially with handsome Jack Colter waiting in the parking lot. After all, Kathy was a silent witness to some interesting photos of Hendersonville's most prominent citizens in comprising romantic photo play with people other than their legally married spouse. Shelby knew she could rely on Kathy's digression and she knew her film had just gone to the head of the line. After all, one never knew who might be captured on film by Hendersonville's prettiest detective.

Kathy looked up to Shelby. "Come back in about 40 minutes Shelby, okay?"

"Perfect," Shelby said with a smile. "I'll see you then, and thank you."

Shelby was very pleased; she'd have them back in less than an hour. Her thoughts returned to the job at hand and away from the handsome Mr. Colter.

Smiling at Jack as she returned, she said, "I'll get my photos back today."

"Good," Jack replied, and drove Shelby back to his mother's home.

Safe at Maggie Colter's house, Jack sat back in the seat and looked long at Shelby.

"I have to check in at the store for a few hours but I'll be back early and I'd like to take you to dinner."

"I'll be ready," Shelby agreed, slipping out of the Bronco. At the moment, she wasn't sure she could handle a romantic goodbye. Agreeing to dinner seemed an easy way out.

His dark eyes sparkled with pleasure and he leaned over for a short kiss.

With a laugh she scooted out of the Ford. She wasn't sure she could bare the soft sensuality of yet another kiss.

Opening the back door, she scooped up the bear and her purchases.

"You owe me," he said in a low friendly growl. She knew quite well what he meant.

Watching him drive away, she sighed, felt emotionally drained.

"How was the Parkway?" Maggie said, coming out onto the porch. Shelby shook her head. Maggie must have watched them drive up and had stayed discreetly behind one of her flowing white window curtains.

Putting her fists squarely on her small hips, Shelby looked at Maggie.

"Maggie, I think this has gone far enough. We really need to tell Jack who I really am."

"Oh no, not just yet dear, he'll be awfully mad," Maggie said in a sugary voice, begging Shelby to understand.

Shelby pounced on Maggie's words. "Maggie! Jack might be in serious danger. We have to tell him and to be honest; I'm not good at lying."

With a glean in her eye, Maggie smiled. "Nonsense dear, I have every bit of faith in you. We'll tell him at the right time."

"Oh look, what do you have there? A little bear, how cute," Maggie said, completely changing the subject. She had completely side stepped the issue. One would never guess, at least by Maggie's demeanor, that her son was in danger.

Shelby frowned.

"Now tell me, dearest, has Jack set another date with you? This is all so exciting."

"Yes," Shelby stammered, "I mean no. Today wasn't a date it was surveillance, Maggie."

"Let me fix you a nice cool glass of tea," Maggie said, opening the porch screen for Shelby. "I want to hear all about your day."

"Maggie, I really...."

"Oh, and here," Maggie said in a hushed whisper, "I made a key to the house so that you can come and go as you please. It's on the dining room table."

"Maggie, you shouldn't be making a key for house guests."

"It's okay, Shelby, I trust you," Maggie replied lightly, "besides you are bonded and licensed. I checked. So when are you seeing Jack again?"

"Tonight, Jack wants to take me," Shelby stopped and looked Maggie squarely in the eyes. "That is, Jack wants to take us to dinner. So, you're going to have to come with us Maggie. I insist!"

Maggie began gathering her purse and car keys along with a couple of envelopes from a table by the door. "Oh sweetie, I just remembered, I have to get these envelopes to the post office."

"Key is on the table, diet soda and tea are in the refrigerator, help yourself dear," Maggie said, deftly making her escape.

"Maggie!" Shelby cried in exasperation. "We have to talk. NOW! No more lies. Jack is well...interested in me. We have to tell him the truth."

"We'll talk about this when I get home," Maggie replied. With a wave, she left Shelby standing alone in the middle of the foyer.

Feeling more frustrated than she had in years, Shelby glanced at her watch. It was almost time to pick up the photos. She went upstairs and dropped off her bags, depositing the bear in a chair by the vanity. Before leaving the house, she found the key Maggie had made for her and she called Chris who was on duty. He agreed to meet her at Eckerd's. He was there waiting.

She waved hello and hurried into the drug store and paid for her photos. Kathy was noncommittal as she gave Shelby her change and her envelope. Shelby guessed Kathy was disappointed with the developed prints, but she thanked her anyway.

"That's them," Shelby said, showing the photos to Chris in his squad car.

"Hum," Chris drawled, suspiciously looking at one half of Jack Colter's blurred head covering half the shot. "I think I recognize this guy. It's hard to tell with half his forehead head and nose in the frame. Is Jack's nose really that big?"

To Shelby's instant displeasure, Chris shuffled through the photos not bothering to hide his snicker at Jack's various poses.

Chris didn't bother to hide his chuckle.

"Oh hush up," Shelby said, trying to keep her temper in check with her former partner. "Jack thought I was taking pictures of him. Now look beyond Jack, you can clearly see the two men by the truck, do you recognize them?"

Chris stopped teasing her and studied the two men in the background of the photos. "No, I don't think I have seen them before. I'll run these photos through the computer and see what we come up with."

"You will call me, right?"

"I'll call you," Chris promised, "but if we identify them, Shelby, you know this might turn into police business sooner rather than later."

"Trust me," she assured him, "I'll happily turn this case over to HPD."

Chris laughed, this time his whole body shook. "So how is the life of a famous romance novelist?"

Thinking of Jack's warm smile, his soft brown eyes, and arms that made her feel safe, she answered, "More dangerous than you could ever imagine. I'll be happy to go back to chasing cheating husbands."

Chris snickered as she got out of the squad car.

"Thanks for the pictures; I'll let you know if anything comes up. Want me on tonight?"

"Go home and get some rest," Shelby said, "I'll be staying with Maggie Colter again tonight. The three of us are going to dinner."

"Did I mention that my wife thinks you and Jack would make a really cute couple?"

"Really?" came Shelby's quick retort, "I don't see that happening. Besides, Jack thinks I'm a romance novelist. I have every confidence that when he finds out

I'm a private investigator, he'll hit the roof."

Chris's grunted, "See your point. Look, I'll call you if I find out anything."

"Thanks," Shelby said as she left the police cruiser.

Returning to her Chevy Tracker, she sat looking at the other photos she had held in her hand. The pictures were taken of the skyline, the waterfall, and their honeymoon shot at the Pisgah Inn taken by they tourist.

It was too easy to have the day and she shivered with each vivid recollection. Looking at the laughter in his cool blue eyes, she tenderly traced his lips remembering the taste of his mouth, the heavenly warmth of his arms. His fresh mountain scent lingered with her like a favorite perfume. She could still sense the protective feel of his hand and the hardness of his muscular chest.

She swallowed hard. Each photo played with her emotions. While she gloried in some, sadness shadowed others. He looked like he was falling in love with her. Was she falling in love with him? Impossible, she chided herself, they're just photos, don't read anything more in his eyes. Ready to tuck them back into the envelope, she stopped at the last picture. It was one of Jack taken when he hadn't been looking. Without meaning to the picture she had taken had captured his intensity, his powerful athletic frame, and his oneness with the untamed wilderness.

"You're one handsome man, Jack Colter, " she said with a long wistful sigh. Her stomach turned, churned with anxiety and frustration. She stared at the picture and with no one to ever hear her, she said, "I almost wish I had met you sooner, when I had a heart to give."

The moment was hurt and Shelby found herself almost wishing she was a romance novelist, and she had the right to fall for Jack Colter.

Pushing the pictures inside the envelope, she stared out the window. She bit her lip and reminded herself, with love came the pain of betrayal.

At that moment a young mother came out of the Eckerd's Drug Store. She was tenderly holding a baby. The chubby infant was cooing, smiling, and the mother was playfully returning soft noises to her child.

Jack would give you beautiful babies a distant voice whispered to her heart.

"I told you," she said for no one to hear. "I can't think about Jack now or ever. I tried love before and it doesn't work for me. Go torment someone else."

Before returning to the Colter residence, Shelby drove by her home. She retrieved the mail from her post office, which included two checks, one from an attorney and another from a grateful client.

It was sobering to return back to her home and she was glad she did. It grounded her and provided her with a much needed respire to sort through her thoughts. She duly watered the plants, checked her email, responded to two online friends, and deleted the jokes her friend Tiffany was fond of sending her. The short time spent alone surround by her own things, reminding her of who she was and would always be gave her a renewed sense of strength and resolve.

Tonight, she vowed, Maggie or no, she would tell Jack tonight and get this assignment on track. Picking an outfit suitable for dinner, she decided to save her shower until later and hurried back to Maggie's house.

It was almost five when she returned to the Colter house. Maggie had returned, at least her car was parked behind the house though she was nowhere to be found. She was either resting, Shelby mused, or hiding from the inevitable.

If Jack were true to his word and she knew him to be, he had promised her an early dinner and decided to shower and change.

Applying make-up an hour later, she was still trying to justify the care she had taken with her appearance. Her long brown hair was shining. She had a wealth of thick brown hair that tumbled carelessly down her back. She took time to put on some eye shadow before she applied the sable rich mascara that framed her lashes and brought out the color of her blue eyes.

Slipping on the dress she chose she was instantly angry at herself for choosing it. Hardly professional attire, she remembered she had last worn the dress to a cocktail reception of a lawyer friend, but she didn't recall the black spandex dress fitting her so snugly. Scrutinizing her reflection, she was annoyed. The bodice dipped too low for her liking and showed off far too much of her full breasts. The spandex was tight fitting and accented every soft curve she had. What was she thinking when she picked it out, and worse yet, what would Jack be thinking when he saw her in it? It reeked of sexuality, HERS!

Shelby frowned and looking at her reflection in the mirror, she realized she had applied too much red lipstick, but if she tried to wipe it off now, it would only smear it. Her lips looked as if they were begging for a kiss, and she didn't want to give that impression, did she?

Smoothing the dress over her trim hips, there's nothing she could do about this now, as it's the only dress she brought with her.

As she slipped into her small black heels, she would have to make quick work of the evening. Maggie would be there, she thought in no small comfort.

Five minutes later she was standing in the living room.

Jack stood across from her and nearly paled when he saw her. He recovered quickly and his welcoming smile left a cold knot in her stomach. He was definitely attracted to her and she was helpless to stop his fascination.

Shelby returned Jack's smile and nearly jumped to find Maggie dressed in a housecoat, seated with boxes of tissues all around her.

"You look lovely dear," Maggie said, pulling out several tissues in rapid succession. For effect she blew her nose prettily. "I'm afraid I'm coming down with something. I should stay home and rest. You and Jack will have to enjoy yourselves without me."

"What?" Shelby cried. She took a quick breath. "You aren't coming with us?"

"No, no, not tonight, dear," Maggie cooed, fringing two short and very dry coughs.

Shelby was livid. She couldn't be alone with Jack. Not in this dress!

"You look magnificent, Silver," Jack said, placing the drink he was holding on the coffee table. His dark blue eyes flashed over her attire taking in each delicious curve.

Shelby could feel her cheeks color. Maggie was practically beaming.

Her body stiffened in shock as Brad McClannahan came into the living room.

"Here's your tea, Maggie," Brad McClannahan said, placing a cup and saucer next to her. For different reasons it seemed, he also looked at Shelby's appearance and was clearly incensed. He glared at Shelby. "Good evening Ms. Lake, you look charming."

He took a seat next to Shelby and continued to glare at her. His dark interest scanned every inch of her making her skin crawl. Why had he taken such a dislike of her?

"Nice to see you Brad," she said, moving further into the room. Once again Shelby tried to remember from where she knew him. Certainly she should have remembered this large burly man.

Jack came to her side. "It's you and me kid. Brad stopped by a few minutes ago and has promised to stay with Mother."

"I just feel too bad to go out tonight," Maggie whined, sounding oh so innocent. With the fringed fragility of a woman twice her age, she brought the teacup helplessly to her lips.

Maggie may have fooled both men, but Shelby was hardly taken in by Maggie's sudden illness.

"You two run along," Maggie urged them, making a faint attempt to hide her smile. "I'm going to get Brad to run out shortly for some dinner for us. Have a good time."

Under Brad's glare, and behind Maggie's mischievous smile, for one moment, Shelby thought of blurting out the truth. Didn't these people realize they were in mortal danger? She quickly assessed the situation. Jack's eyes were soft and warm on her.

"Jack, why don't you bring Ms. Lake out to the field tomorrow?" Brad said suddenly sounding strangely exhilarated, "I can give her a bird's eye view of Hendersonville. I'm sure it will help her with her research."

"Oh, that won't be necessary," Shelby assured him. Though not given to premonitions, she had the clear image of her body, without a parachute, being hurled from Brad's plane.

"No, I insist," Brad said a little too forcefully.

Maggie took another sip of her tea. "Silver, there's nothing to worry about. Brad's an excellent pilot."

R-i-g-h-t, Shelby thought to herself, realizing she had a whole twelve hours or more to think of a way out of this unwelcome excursion. She wasn't about to tell Brad McClannahan she was morbidly afraid of flying.

"Well, I have made dinner reservations at The Grove Park Inn Resort & Spa, Silver. It's one of Asheville's most beautiful restaurants. Perhaps you've heard of it?"

Shelby smiled, she hadn't thought of a location for dinner. The Grove Park Inn in Asheville was perfect. The likelihood of running into anyone she knew would be remote. She was pleased.

All was not lost, she thought hopefully. Her secret identity would be safe until morning. That's what you thought today, a small voice reminded her with the image of Red Chandler coming to mind.

Nonsense, she argued with herself, what could possibly go wrong? The mission then was to go to dinner, eat as fast as she could, and return home. She could handle that.

"Well, if we don't leave now we'll miss our reservation," Jack said. "Pretty lady, are you ready to go?"

There was nothing to do but allow Jack to escort her out to his Bronco. With Brad in tow, Maggie followed them.

Brad would keep Maggie safe. Jack was with her. There was nothing she needed to do except enjoy the evening.

Weaving through the neighborhood, Jack was quickly out to Highway 25, onto Interstate 26, and headed toward Asheville.

"Have you been to The Grove Park Inn Resort & Spa before?"

"No," Shelby lied. Lying was becoming easier all the time.

"It was built in 1913 and is clearly one of the most famous and distinctive of the grand hotels in the south. If traffic stays as light, we'll be able to take in the sunset. When the sun goes down you'll be treated to a breathtaking view of the Asheville skyline and the Blue Ridge Mountains. I assure you there is no more beautiful or romantic place in Asheville than The Grove Park Inn. I know you'll like it."

"It sounds lovely," Shelby said thoughtfully, not sure whether she could endure one more romantic or magical moment with this handsome man.

Even nature was conspiring against her as the saffron sky had taken on a deeper shade of cadmium orange. Long chars of violet, peach, and dusky fell from the sky kissing the distant mountain with spectacular light.

The traffic remained light into Asheville with slight exception at the Interstate 26 and the I-40 interchange. They drove across the wide expanse of the French Broad River and into the downtown area before exiting to Charlotte Street.

All too quickly they had arrived at The Grove Park Inn Resort & Spa. It truly was magnificent but then she and everyone who lived in western North Carolina were aware of that.

The Grove Park Inn Resort & Spa was elegant, timeless in its stature, and would prove to be a safe haven for a quiet evening meal with Jack Colter. Shelby was well pleased with the choice as a valet parking attendant graciously opened the door the very moment the vehicle stopped.

A second attendant handed Jack a receipt, which he tucked into his shirt pocket. With a voice soft in warmth, he said, "Shall we?"

She smiled and felt a sense of relaxation sweep through her body. She was safe. Safe. Safe. Safe.

Two steps into the lobby, she froze and read with horror 'Welcome North Carolina Law Enforcement Association.'

Across from her, the Great Hall bar was filled to capacity with friends, fellow law enforcement officers, just about everyone she knew! She brought her hand in front of her mouth to muffle a cry.

Shelby considered her choices, run for her life, hide or both. Instead, she stood immobile taking in the 300 plus members of the law enforcement community. In microseconds she counted the last moments of her secret identity.

"Looks a bit crowded honey," she heard Jack whisper. His voice sounded miles away. Why couldn't her feet move?

"I had no idea it would be this crowded tonight," Jack said softly.

Shelby felt the knot in her stomach and her mouth was suddenly dry. She gulped and knew her eyes were as wide as saucers. "Me either."

"If it's all right with you, let's go straight to the restaurant. I'm sure this group will be moving to one of the banquet rooms shortly. We could have a cocktail later."

"Good idea," Shelby said her voice so hoarse it was barely audible even to her own ears.

As they moved away from the Great Hall, Shelby buried her head into Jack's arm hoping her long brown hair hid the exposed part of her face. Her mission, should she try to attempt this gauntlet, was to get to the Sunset Terrace as quickly as possible.

As they reached the beautiful Sunset Terrace, a lovely hostess appeared and politely tried to ignore Shelby who was doing a poor job of hiding beside Jack. Without breaking her serene composure, the hostess smiled and motioned them to follow her through the restaurant.

Still clutching Jack's arm, Shelby followed her through the restaurant.

Reaching the table, Shelby nearly collapsed into her seat and lifted the oversized menu in front of her.

"Good evening. My name is Carrie Ann; it's my pleasure to serve you this evening," a young college student introduced herself. "Could I get you something to drink while you look at your menus?"

"Bourbon and water for me," Jack replied.

Sinking low in her seat, Shelby nervously glanced about the restaurant and said to Carrie Ann, "White wine. Hurry!"

Positioning herself behind the oversized menu, she slouched, hoping it hid her body. This wasn't so bad, she mused, and I could manage a quick meal from this position.

With the outstanding service The Grove Park Inn Resort & Spa was internationally known for, the drinks arrived in record time.

Shelby would have loved to enjoy some of the Sunset Terrace Chophouse wonderfully prepared appetizers, her favorites being the Blackened Crab Cakes and the Portobello Savory Tart but knew better than to prolong the meal with a delicious appetizer. Keep it simple, she told herself then added privately, yeah, look where that had gotten her.

"I think I will have the Sun Tried Tomato Caesar Salad," Shelby heard Jack say as he apparently handed the menu to the waitress. "And a New York Strip."

"Very good, "the waitress said before turning to Shelby. "Have you decided yet? I can give you more time."

From behind the menu, Shelby downed the glass of white wine and passed the waitress back her empty glass.

"I'll have the Hearts of Palm Salad with the eight ounce Filet." Shelby said. "And another glass of white wine, hurry."

"Would you care for our signature Steak sauces?"

"Tempting," Jack said with a laugh, "but the New York Strip is perfect as it is."

"Miss, would you care for one of our signature steak sauces."

"Yes, I'd like the cognac-mushroom sauce for me."

"Very good," the waitress said as she gave a soft tug at the menu, but Shelby jerked back, almost toppling back in her chair. Carrie Ann gave Shelby the win. Carrie Ann accepted the empty glass Shelby had passed to her.

"I'll bring you another glass of wine," she sniffed as she hurried away.

Jack cleared his throat. "Darling, I'd much rather look at your pretty face than the back of that menu."

Shelby heard the confusion in his voice and she slowly lowered the menu just enough to made a quick scan of the room.

The waitress returned with Shelby's second glass of wine and stretched out her hand, insisting on the menu. Shelby had no choice but to surrender it. With the prized menu in hand, the young waitress gave Shelby an odd gaze but without further comment, left to wait on another table.

Shelby brought both of her hands up to cover her face and peaked around the room through her fingers. She saw no one she knew and ignored the tourists staring at her.

For the first time since she entered The Grove Park Inn, she took a deep breath. Though not out of the woods yet, she was safe and sound for the moment.

Jack sat looking curiously at her. There were touches of humor around his eyes and near his mouth but he never once broke into a smile.

"Is everything all right?" he asked softly.

Shelby nervously pushed back a strand of hair from her face and cleared her throat.

"Of course," she stammered as the waitress returned with the salads. Thankfully, no one she knew was in the restaurant. Though she was not far from harm's way, she realized for the moment she was safe. She shifted in her chair and positioned herself precariously close to the edge of her seat, in position to dive under the table, if she needed to, should circumstances turn against her.

Jack's face reflected a look of bewilderment but he said nothing.

"I need to study this a bit longer, you know, research for the book," Shelby explained.

Jack's eyes lit with understanding and he smiled.

At that moment, Shelby heard the large movement of people out of the Great Hall to the banquet area on the floor below. Apparently the Annual North Carolina Law Enforcement dinner meeting had begun.

With a sigh of relief, she began to relax.

"You may find this interesting. Many famous people have stayed here through the years, Silver," Jack commented as he sliced a tomato on his salad plate. "Houdini, the famous magician, F. Scott Fitzgerald, and seems like I remember Daniel Day Lewis when they were filming the *Last of the Mohicans*. And now, of course, they'll have to add Silver Lake."

"Oh please," she reminded him. "I'm traveling incognito."

Jack nodded. "The Grove Park Inn has its own resident ghost, the Pink Lady."

"Oh," Shelby replied, wondering if she was going to make it out alive.

Shelby finished her salad in record time. Pushing the salad bowl away from her, she waited impatiently for the Filet. The sooner she ate, the sooner they'd leave.

As promised by the evening sky, the sunset was breathtaking with brilliant hues of pink, teal, blue and orange. The sun, in no rush, slid down from the sapphire sky allowing the soft blue of the night sky to follow in its path.

It grew cool on the Terrace and the lights of downtown Asheville sparkled like multicolored gems, sparkling against the night sky.

When their main entrees arrived, Shelby was calm enough to enjoy some semblance of conversation and small talk dominated the meal. In the end, Shelby found she was enjoying both the restaurant and the handsome man seated across from her.

With dinner complete, and their table cleared, the waitress returned with Jack's credit card receipt and a smile. Shelby was certain he had given her a generous tip. His aspect of his personality pleased her.

Shelby smiled and gathered her small handbag before allowing him to lead her out of the restaurant and back through the Great Hall bar. Thankfully, it was nearly empty when they walked through a moment later.

"How about a night cap?" Jack offered.

"If you don't mind," Shelby answered with a nervous glance about the Great Hall, "it's been a long day, and I would just like to go home."

The exit awaited her like the goal line of an indoor track finish line. A few more steps and she would exit the building unscathed.

Reaching the doors, Shelby almost fainted with relief.

"Wait here, Jack cooed to her, "I'll have valet bring the car."

Watching him leave, Shelby froze as she recognized a familiar voice from behind her.

"Well, if it isn't little Shelby MacGregor," Dave Anderson called out to her, "still keeping the peace in Hendersonville?"

"Hi Dave," Shelby said to her late-arriving friend from Hickory. She lost no time in adding, "Do me a favor, I'm here undercover."

"Undercover?"

"Yes," Shelby pleaded in hushed tones, hoping he would see the desperation in her eyes.

Seeing Jack approach, Dave smiled, spun on his heels, and without another word walked away.

"Was that man bothering you?" Jack said with a glance toward Dave Anderson.

"No, no," Shelby assured him. "He actually saw me on a talk show recently. He said his wife was a fan and he just wanted to say hello."

It was at that moment the valet service returned the Ford Bronco and the valet captain opened the door for Shelby.

Safely in the vehicle, Jack retraced their path through Asheville.

Travel by night always seems faster than day time. Jack was relatively quiet on the ride home no doubt. It wasn't until they pulled into Maggie's driveway that Shelby's heart slowed to normal.

"You amaze me, Silver," Jack continued as turned off the engine. "You're a brilliant and talented writer yet modesty keeps you from mentioning any of your successful books."

Not modesty, Shelby thought in silent reply, I just don't know any of 'my' books.

"You are soft, feminine, smart, a fantastic cook, and your books are filled with your passion. You are truly an amazing woman," Jack said, looking at her. "I really want to tell you how much I've enjoyed your company today."

Shelby turned away from him. Her face colored remembering the erotic books Silver Lake had penned. Looking at Maggie's dark house she couldn't help but realize how Shelby MacGregor paled to the accomplishments and virtues of Silver Lake.

She turned back to him and smiled. "Thank you Jack and I want to thank you again for this lovely day. You've been an excellent guide."

The moon was now fully up in the western Carolina sky and the stars began to shine like diamonds around it.

Brad's Lincoln pulled into the driveway behind them.

"Oh look," Jack's voice rose in surprise. "My mother and Brad are behind us. Good, she must be feeling better."

"How was dinner?" Brad said, coming up behind them. He glared angrily at Shelby. "Ms Lake, I hope you enjoyed yourself?"

"Yes, I did," Shelby answered him as pleasantly as she could, "it was lovely."

"Well, I'm the big winner tonight," Maggie shouted, emerging from the car. "I won the jackpot, $ 50.00."

Shelby frowned. "Oh good, I guess after we left you started feeling better."

Without a shadow of guilt, Maggie cheerfully replied, "Oh yes, don't know what came over me. One minute I was sick as a dog and the next, well, I felt better.

Brad suggested we go play Bingo and we did. Gee, I wish I could have joined you and Jack but I'm sure you had a lovely time without me."

"Bingo," Shelby muttered under her breath.

"Well, you two look like you had a grand time," Maggie said to both Jack and Shelby. "Now, I made some homemade lemonade this afternoon. Why don't you and Silver go rest on the porch? Brad, would you give me a hand?"

Brad followed Maggie into the house. Jack and Shelby positioned themselves on the swing when Maggie and Brad returned with the ice cold lemonade. Maggie then took her favorite seat in a white rocker and Brad sat close to her in a wicker chair.

Maybe it was the light midsummer breeze that was both fresh and sweet, maybe it was the easy laughter as Jack and Maggie shared tales of growing up, or the simple sweetness of the homemade lemonade, but Shelby began to feel at peace.

She was sure their soft laughter could be heard about the neighborhood. One hour stretched into another and another until all were trying to hide their yawns.

"Oh my it's time for bed, and time for my medicine," Maggie said, looking at her watch. Rising from the glider, she wished everyone a goodnight and added, "Brad, stay as long as you wish, but I'm going to bed."

Brad rose to his feet and gave Maggie a quick hug. "No, no, it's long past my bedtime too."

With a daring glance at Shelby, he added coldly, "Besides, Jack is bringing out Silver to the airfield tomorrow."

"That's so kind of you to offer," Shelby said, trying to keep her voice even. "But I assure you, it's absolutely unnecessary."

"Nonsense!" Brad countered, his dark look turning to black. "I'm sure you will find it very fascinating, I know I will."

Maggie said goodnight again and unexpectedly gave both Jack and Shelby a hug.

Wishing she truly was a part of this family, Shelby savored the sweetness of the moment.

As Brad's Lincoln drove away, Shelby heard the sounds of Maggie climbing the stairs to her bedroom. Still, she sat with Jack, his hand cupping hers, his thigh so close it felt like a second skin. Each long breath he took drew brought both serenity and stirring desire from deep within her.

Exhausted from the day's events, she was tired, but at this moment never felt so alive and so real. She was intoxicated with his nearness. She didn't want to leave him and leave this night. He likewise seemed reluctant to go.

"Thank you for today," she said softly.

He pulled her close to him and wrapped his arms about her. For a long moment he just held her.

He brought his lips down to hers. She felt her arms gently wrapping them about his narrow waist and her body melting into his.

In his arms, the world ceased to be. She ceased to be, her spirit, her soul lost in his embrace.

What started as a sweet goodnight kiss grew deeper and turned passionate. Waves of ecstasy rushed through her, flooding her with higher levels of desire. Her defenses were weakening and she knew she needed him all the more. She knew she could never get close enough to this wonderful man.

When at last, they reluctantly parted; his eyes were dark upon her.

"I don't want to leave you tonight," he said softly.

"I know," she said missing him, and he hadn't even left her side.

Reluctantly they parted, this time not from fear of the future, but of sadness of the night.

"It doesn't feel right being apart from you," Jack said, the huskiness in his voice that betrayed the ache from deep inside him.

After a long pause, he pushed her away from him. "You need to rest."

She nodded back at him without speaking.

With a soft kiss to her lips he turned and walked down the porch. Stopping at the steps, he turned and looked back at her. With a smile, he said, "Goodnight Silver Lake, sweet dreams."

She waved and smiled back. "Sweet dreams, Jack."

He stared at her, studying her features as if to keep the image then for a final time and descended the steps to head toward his dark house.

Like a schoolboy he turned and smiled again. She was no better, watching him until he disappeared into the shadows.

With her heart pounding, she quietly left the porch and took care in closing the door. She silently turning the lock for in her mind alone, any sound at all would somehow break the magic spell she was under.

Upstairs Shelby noticed Maggie's light was off. Quietly she went to her room without bothering to turn on a light and slid out of the dress in the darkness. A quick splash of cold water to her face did little to bring her back to reality, and she wasn't sure if she wanted to return.

Changing into a pair of gray sweat pants and white t-shirt, she giggled. Fans everywhere certainly imagined Silver Lake in a pink negligee resting on a satin round bed surrounded by dozens of toy poodles or white fluffy cats.

She hardly dressed the part of Silver Lake, but then she wasn't Silver Lake. She was Shelby MacGregor and Jack Colter was falling for her. She could see it in his eyes; she could feel it in her heart.

Ignoring the whimsical emotions and muddled thoughts, she mechanically found her gun still safe in her purse and placed it beside her on the nightstand. She had visions of repeating this process with Jack beside her and giggled again curious as to the look in his eyes.

With her window open, and the sweet fragrances of honeysuckle and magnolia drifting into her room, she fell into a peaceful sleep until; she heard the crystal clear sound of glass breaking.

She was instantly awake, her hand reaching her revolver before her feet had hit the floor. The adrenaline rush instantaneous as years of police work checked any misplaced alarm.

The room was dark, and she moved quickly to the door. She heard the second sound of glass, not shattering but being rattled as if swept away from a window pane. It was outside of the house.

Sliding into the hallway, the door to Maggie's room was still shut and no light was seeping from it. Maggie was still asleep.

She moved slowly down the hall, listening for sounds of an unknown stranger. The house was quiet.

A bit delayed, she heard the loud barking of a neighborhood dog. Someone was outside the house.

With her gun lowered, she carried it in both hands and prepared to bring the heavy glock up in an instant.

Passing through the dining room, she saw the light in Jack's bedroom come on and knew the disturbance had awakened him. Making her way through the kitchen, she eased past the table. Her every sense alert.

Reaching the door, she brought the gun to her face, the trigger a hair's distance from her lips. Its coldness giving her a strange comfort. Slowly, she turned the lock and opened the door. Slipping out into the darkness, she eased the door shut behind her.

The moon had left the sky, and the stars offered only dim light.

She heard the heavy sound of footsteps moving in soft underbrush. The sound was distinctive. She realized it was not in Maggie's yard but from Jack's shadowy yard.

Jack!

She heard the sound of someone moving closer to her.

With her heart racing, she waited in the darkness. Slowly, she pulled the hammer back and locked it with her thumb.

The danger was quick upon her. She brought her weapon down slightly. Her arms outstretched, it was now even with her shoulder. The gun was firmly balanced in her small hands. Her every sense alert to rhythm of steady movement drawing nearer. Without fear, she stepped into the sound ready to fire.

CHAPTER SEVEN

F reeze," a familiar voice demanded.
For one instant, gun drawn, she held her piece on Chris Turner.

In his police uniform, Chris held the gun steady for a half second before lowering it to his side.

"Shelby!" he cried in a hoarse whisper. "I nearly shot you."

"You didn't," she responded in a cool voice, keeping her gaze steady. With ice spreading through her stomach and her limbs, the glock felt heavy to hold. She brought it to her side grateful she hadn't fired. Swallowing hard, her mouth was dry and she felt small moist sweat beads form on the top of her lips. She had almost shot her former partner in the chest.

Chris offered her a lopsided grin. "You could have killed me."

"Yeah," she managed, feeling her knees beginning to buckle under her. She could have. Years of training had stopped both of them from firing. They looked at one another and smiled

Chris spoke first. "You okay?"

Shelby nodded her head as she heard the back screen door open.

"Who's there?" Jack Colter demanded his voice chilled with anger.

Ignoring Jack for the briefest of moments, she looked at

Chris and in a hushed tone asked, "What are you doing here? I thought you were off tonight."

"I was," Chris said under his breath. "Then one of the guys called in sick, you didn't need me so I offered to take his place. Jack Colter's alarm went off and his security firm called HPD. I was in the neighborhood, so I took the call."

"I said who's there?" Jack demanded a second time from the other side of the house.

"I'm Officer Chris Turner with the Hendersonville PD, Mr. Colter," Chris called to him. "Your security firm alerted us. Are you all right?"

Whatever Jack said was lost in a voice brimming with anger.

Safe in the shadows, she could do nothing but stare at Chris.

Chris looked over his shoulder and turned back to Shelby. "Whoever broke the window is probably gone. I better go see what's going on with Jack before he comes out here and finds you."

"I'll talk to you in the morning," Shelby said with a nod. "Any news on these guys in the photos I gave you?"

"Nothing yet," Chris said under his breath, then turned and hurried in Jack's direction.

"Are you all right, Mr. Colter?" Chris shouted as he waved goodbye to Shelby.

"Yes," she heard Jack reply. "Watch your step, there's glass everywhere. Someone busted the window on my back door."

Shelby leaned back against the corner of the building and took in a breath.

Chris stepped fully into the light.

"Another car is on the way, sir," Chris said as he walked around the corner to where Jack must have been standing.

"Is there anyway you can stop anyone else from coming?" Jack snapped, "I don't want a bunch of police cars swarming my house. Nothing has been taken; the alarm scared them off. Probably just a bunch of kids anyway."

"Mr. Colter," she heard Chris' reply, "do you mind I come in and take a look around?"

Shelby heard Chris' heavy shoes climb the steps to the back entrance of the house. Their voices were now muffled. Both men were safe in Jack's house.

Taking in slow breaths, Shelby rested against the side of the house.

For a half second, she thought of marching into Jack's house and blurting out everything, warning him of the danger he was in. Now was not the time.

Jack was upset and probably agitated. Besides, she told herself, neither she nor the police department had concrete evidence that anything was going on.

The break-in could have been a bunch of kids with nothing else to do as Jack suggested, but Shelby doubted it for any number of reasons. To have reached the back of Jack's house they would have passed by numerous glass doors and windows in the neighborhood that would have proven much easier picking, and to have gotten to the back of Jack's house from the road, they would have had to come down his long driveway risking exposure.

Why had someone gone to the trouble of breaking out the window, only to have left?

The grass beneath her was damp and it made her bare feet cold and uncomfortable.

Despite Jack's protest, other law enforcement officers would be arriving as a matter of policy. There was nothing she could do but return to Maggie's house before she was discovered.

She quickly retraced her steps and as she closed the kitchen door, she watched a second police car pull up behind Chris' cruiser. For the moment, Jack was safe.

In Maggie's kitchen, she locked the door as quietly as possible before going to the second floor to check on Maggie. She slowly opened the door.

The room was dark but she could easily make out Maggie sleeping in the middle of her bed. Her breathing was steady. There was no need to wake her.

Shelby quietly closed the door and returned to her bedroom.

Though Jack's house was not visible from her window, she stared out her window to the garden below. In the morning, she and Maggie would tell Jack the truth.

She returned to bed as the grandfather clocked chimed three.

Drifting off to an uneasy sleep, she thought she heard the police cars leave and glanced at the red illuminated numbers on her clock. It read 4:28. She closed her eyes.

It seemed almost the next moment someone was knocking at her door.

It was quarter after eight.

"Shelby," Maggie squealed, peeking into her room.

She yawned and Maggie took her stretch as an open invitation to enter.

"Oh good, you're awake," Maggie said breathlessly. Her eyes were sparkling and her grin contagious. Dressed in a short sleeve pink blouse and a stylish pair of beige pants, she squealed, "You won't believe what happened last night! And to think I slept right through it!"

In spite of herself, Shelby smiled. How dare bedlam occur without Maggie's small hand to mastermind it? Her face was alive with excitement.

"It's Jack!" Maggie said, flaying her arms wildly about. "Someone tried to break into his house last night."

Shelby let out a long, audible breath. "Maggie, I know, I was there."

Breathless, Maggie continued, "Jack thinks it was probably a teenage prank or something. Oh my goodness! We have never, never had a robbery or anything else like this in our neighborhood before."

Maggie stopped. She dropped her hands. The melodrama gone, her voice went flat, and she stared at Shelby. "What did you say? You were there? What do you mean you were there? When?"

"Last night, of course," Shelby said, sitting up in bed. "I heard the glass break and went over to Jack's house. The police were also there. What do the police think?"

"Oh they don't know and Jack won't take this seriously!"

Shelby steadied her gaze. "Maggie, listen to me, we need to talk to Jack today. And I need to hear whatever you are hiding from me NOW!"

Maggie's eyes widened and she managed to look genuinely surprised.

Her voice rose a full octave as she asked, "Me? Hiding something from you?"

"Yes Maggie," Shelby insisted, keeping a small bit in her words, "the real reason you hired me. I need to know it now!"

Maggie looked at Shelby but said nothing.

There was a tell tale flutter in her eyes. Whatever she was about to say was a lie. "Shelby, dear, I'm not hiding anything from you."

Shelby threw back the covers and stood up.

"Maggie," Shelby began as if she were talking to a child, "there's something else going on here that I don't know about.

137

Something that I need to know. And, we can no longer leave Jack in the dark anymore. His life may be in danger. Is there something you are not telling me? You must tell me. NOW!"

"Nothing dear," Maggie replied, looking about the room, focusing on every corner, knick knack, crevice, and cranny. She was looking at everything but Shelby. Even a child would have known she was lying. "Really, my darling, there is nothing that is being kept from you that in any way would harm either you or my son."

Moving nervously about the room, Maggie added, "And, Shelby, it's more important than ever that Jack doesn't know who you are. Not just yet. By the way, have you learned anything more about the men who were following Jack?"

Shelby replied with a frown. "No, not yet. We should hear something today."

For the first time this morning, Maggie grew strangely serious.

"You mean someone really did break into his home and is trying to harm him? Jack believes it was just a couple of high school kids out for a little prank."

"I don't know what to think Maggie," Shelby replied honestly. "We still don't have anything solid. We've seen a truck with stolen license plates in the neighborhood and last night party or parties unknown broke into Jack's house. One thing I do know, we have to tell Jack about your-our suspicions. Jack needs to become involved in his own safety."

Maggie shook her head.

"Just one more day," she stammered. "I need time to figure this out."

Shelby shook her head. "No, Maggie, today. Today or I will tell him myself."

Maggie nodded. "All right, we'll tell Jack everything this afternoon, I promise on my grandchild's life."

Shelby frowned. "You don't have a grandchild."

Maggie didn't bother to hide her smile. "Well, not yet, that is, well, you know what I mean. I promise we'll tell Jack."

Shelby wasn't happy but she had little choice. This afternoon it would be.

Smoothing out imaginary wrinkles in slacks, Maggie looked toward the door and said, "Jack's already downstairs. He brought us some breakfast. We better go down and eat."

With that Maggie slipped from the room. Shelby frowned. At least she could take some comfort in knowing Jack would know the truth about her and about the men who may or may not be following him. She would leave law enforcement to determine if the break-in was indeed the work of burglars or a childish escapade by a group of maundering teens out too late at night.

Shelby slipped out of her sweats and t-shirt and took time for a shower. Finding a white blouse and white slacks hanging in the closet, she changed into the outfit, touched up her make-up, and hurried down to join Jack and Maggie.

Maggie and Jack were seated at the breakfast table. A variety box of donuts and pastries lay open between them.

Maggie rose and went to the countertop where she brought over a pot of freshly brewed coffee.

Aware her heart fluttered at the mere sight of him, she kept her eyes downcast and added cream and sugar to the coffee.

Jack folded the newspaper and stared at her. She saw the heart rendering tenderness in his gaze and her heart jumped unexpectedly. If there was any doubt he was falling for her, it was gone. "Good morning, beautiful. Did you sleep well?"

Shelby returned his smile trying unsuccessfully to not stare at the sensuous curve of his lips or the warmth in his electric blue eyes. His eyes warmed her and she wondered with a sharp intake of breath would he still look so sweetly at her when he knew she was a P.I., not a romance novelist.

She quickly took in the light blue polo shirt that accentuated his powerful chest and shoulders, its sleeves breaking off just at his muscular biceps. He looked kissable and she wanted to kiss him.

"Your mother told me your home was broken into last night," Shelby said with a frown. Maggie offered her a chocolate éclair. Shelby shook her head, she hadn't exercised in three days and she couldn't afford the delicacy.

"I'd hardly call someone throwing a rock into my kitchen a break-in," Jack scoffed, pushing the paper away from him. He seemed intent on focusing his attention wholly on her. Shelby caught a glimpse of Maggie trying to hide a smile.

"Really? What would you call it?" Shelby said, trying to avoid his steady gaze.

"It was nothing," his voice assured her. His eyes were focused on her lips. Leaning back into his chair, he added, "A bunch of teenagers out having a bit of fun. The burglar alarm went off; the police arrived within minutes then end of story."

Shelby took a sip of coffee more certain than ever that Jack had no regard for his own personal safety. "I take it you have a security system. Good. How about motion detectors? It's always a good to have motion detectors."

Jack shook his head. "None for me. Every time a stray cat slips by at night the yard was flooded with light. Besides, a man should be able to take care of his family."

"Jack dear," Maggie cautioned him, "don't be so macho. You will scare our Silver away."

Jack chuckled and looked devilishly handsome. "Nonsense, Mother, I've taken the time to read several of Silver's novels, I can assure you, she likes her men macho."

Though he was clearly teasing, the mouth full of coffee Shelby had almost spewed across the table instead went down the wrong way causing her to cough violently. Regaining her composure, she offered him a weak smile.

Hiding the rest of her feelings behind her cup of coffee, she wondered what Jack Colter would think of a woman who could take care of herself and him?

"Well, I told Brad I'd have you at the airport by 9:30. Don't you want something to eat before we go?"

A soft gasp escaped her lips as shock flew through her. She had forgotten about the darn plane ride. "What? It's today? Today!"

Jack looked momentarily confused as if he had been expecting her to be happy.

Maggie reached for another sugared donut. Between bites, she said, "Brad would be terribly disappointed if you changed your mind, Silver."

"And," Jack added with a chuckle, "as an accomplished pilot yourself, I know you'll enjoy this."

Shelby felt panic rising inside her. Her stomach twisted and her breaths were coming in short shallow gasps. Her fear of flying was consuming every nerve of her body. She colored fiercely and only half listened as Jack began telling her about what she would see.

Perhaps this singular treat would thrill the high flying Ms. Silver Lake, but Shelby sat, too stunned to move or even breath.

The only bright thought was that Brad McClannahan actually would push her out of his plane.

"Silver dear," Maggie said suddenly, pulling her attention away from her imaginary fall. "I'm sure you will enjoy this short flight."

"I don't think so," Shelby hissed though her teeth.

Jack rose from the table. "Well, we better get going. I'll go get my car."

The instant Jack was out of the door, Shelby wheeled toward Maggie. Her hands were shaking as she hit the tabletop with her small fists.

"I'm not getting into that darn plane, Maggie. I'm afraid of flying!"

"Really?" Maggie said with a look of surprise. "Brad is expecting you and Jack thinks you're Silver Lake. Oh Shelby, you'll simply have to go."

"No," Shelby cried in promise. "Absolutely not, besides Brad McClannahan hates me."

"Nonsense," Maggie replied as if she were talking to a child, "Brad is the sweetest man I know. He wouldn't hurt a fly."

Shelby laughed. "HA! If looks could kill Maggie, I'd have been a dead woman the night he saw me. Trust me, there's no doubt in my mind he would wring my neck if he had half a chance. I'm sure of that."

Maggie laughed. "You're being a silly-nilley. Brad is the sweetest, kindest man I know. Besides, you'll be up and down before you know it. Brad is an excellent pilot. He's been flying for years."

"Ready?" Jack said, returning to the kitchen.

"I'm not getting on that plane, Maggie," Shelby hissed in a low growl, at the same time allowing Maggie to help her from the table.

With a wink, Maggie whispered, "You'll have a wonderful time."

"No, I won't," Shelby promised.

Maggie offered her a charming smile. Shelby felt her resolve weakening.

Not wanting to argue with Maggie in front of Jack, she relented, the Colter house was fifteen minutes away from the airfield. She had plenty of time to come up with an expectable excuse before she arrived.

"We'll tell Jack everything this afternoon, I promise, "Maggie said, giving her a quick hug. "I just need you to be Silver Lake a few more hours. Please?"

"All right, all right, all right," Shelby agreed, her heart squeezing in anguish. "But we will tell Jack everything today!"

Maggie's face flooded with relief. She gave Shelby a second hug. "Now, run along you two," Maggie said loud enough for Jack to hear, "you'll have a wonderful time!"

For half a second Shelby stood, debating whether she should tack on an additional charge for her hazardous duty. Fighting criminals was one thing, being in a plane was another.

Walking to Jack's SUV, Shelby once again tried to remember when or where she had met Brad McClannahan. They must have a connection somewhere, where?

Jack opened the vehicle's door and she got in. He gallantly closed it behind her.

Her cell phone rang as Jack slid behind the driver's seat. Shelby glanced at the number; it was Chris.

"My agent," she said to Jack.

"Can you talk?" Chris asked.

"Not really," she stammered.

"Okay," Chris replied, "then listen. We combed the area last night. No tire tracks, nothing. Jack thinks it was a bunch of kids."

"I'm aware of that," Shelby said, shifting in her seat.

"Have you spoken to the Chief yet?" she asked. Noticing Jack glance, she quickly added, "The Chief Publisher?"

"He's aware you're watching the Colters. I'm afraid we're as much in the dark about this as you are. I'll tell you this Shelby; I'm with you. Something is going to happen. We just don't know what or when."

Shelby once again had the hunch that Maggie's secret agenda was the clue to solving this mystery, but she could hardly voice her thoughts at the moment.

"Any news on the photos?" she asked, stumbling over her words, "I mean the photo layout."

"We are supposed to hear something mid morning. Where will you be?"

With her mouth dry she replied, "Oh, up about 15,000 feet over Hendersonville. Brad McClannahan, a friend of the Colters, has offered to give me a bird's eye view of Hendersonville."

Chris howled with laughter. "Have you told anyone you are afraid to fly?"

"No can do," Shelby explained with a nervous glance to Jack. She still had to get out of this fiasco as Jack was turning into the airport.

Chris was practically snorting with laughter.

"Glad you think this is so funny," Shelby hissed into the cell.

"It's hilarious!" Chris agreed. "Look, I'll call you when we get the report in. Have a safe trip!"

He ended the call before she could shriek at him.

The call lasted too long. Jack pulled into a parking space at the airport.

The Hendersonville Airfield was not a commercial airport or even a regional hub, but rather a small grassy strip of land, which privately owned small aircraft were tethered to either side of the runway. It served the airplane enthusiasts, retired pilots, and some small businessmen who preferred the airstrip to the larger Asheville Airport.

A large hanger dominated the airport and amassed airplane memorabilia. It was the base where pilots and retirees gathered to drink coffee and remember old times.

Brad was standing to the next to the hanger when he saw Jack approach. He said something to his companions and walked to Jack's Bronco.

"I thought you two had might have had other plans," Brad called out in greeting.

"We got a little delayed. Last night a couple of kids broke the glass in my back door."

"Oh," Brad said with concern, "come on and tell me on the way."

Jack told Brad about the break-in and Brad's rapid inquiries gave her no polite way to enter the conversation. With her mouth dry as cotton and her palms sweaty, she had no recourse but to follow them.

As he finished his tale, the men stopped in front of a very small plane.

"So Silver, what do you think?" Brad asked suddenly.

Shelby had nothing to say.

His Cessna Skyhawk was sleek with well-defined lines. White with yellow accents, the Cessna sat ready for take off. Though there appeared to be ample leg room, she had no intention of setting a foot inside that aircraft.

A malicious smile curled both sides of Brad's mouth as he said, "Would you like to do the ground check before we take off?"

The cold look in his eyes should have sent her running, but Shelby stood her ground.

"Why?" she asked hopefully, "is there anything wrong?"

"Not at all," Brad chuckled with a sarcastic glean in his eyes, "just routine. Jack, would you please help our Ms. Lake into the cockpit."

Jack, ahead of her, opened the Cessna's door, and with his hand tucked under Shelby's elbow practically lifted her onto the seat.

"I don't think this is a good idea," she stammered, but Jack gave her a magical smile, his blue eyes sparkling with pleasure.

"Nonsense, you'll have a wonderful time."

Digging her fingernails into his shirt she allowed him to buckle her into the seat.

"I can sit in the back," she offered, feeling her lungs collapse. She began to hyperventilate. Why didn't he notice she was scared out of her wits?

Brad got in on the other side and began to snap switches overhead and on the dash.

Jack took a step back from the plane just to look at her.

Seeing his faith in her, she tried to steady her breath. She had flown before, never with a madman, and she had flown on a very, very large plane. This would be different. It was only going to be twenty minutes. She could handle twenty minutes. Jack would be with her. No harm would come.

All right, she thought, I can do this. I can fly for twenty minutes. Jack would be with her and she knew if he were near he would keep her safe.

Twenty minutes, twenty minutes, she repeated over and over again. I can handle this for twenty minutes. All I have to do is keep my eyes closed!

Securing in the seat, Shelby waited for Jack to climb into the plane, but he closed the door and took an additional step away from the plane as the Cessna engine roared to life.

"I'll see you in a bit, have fun!" Jack said with a wave goodbye.

"What!" Shelby cried. "Aren't you coming with us?"

The engine began to purr.

"Got a bit of an inner ear problem, Silver," Jack shouted over the engine

noise, tapping the side of his head. "Old football injury. You two go on right ahead. Have a good time."

With Jack clear of the aircraft, the Cessna began to move toward the center of the runway.

"Ms. Lake," Brad hissed. "You look a little pale."

"I'm not feeling well," Shelby grumbled. "This was a bad mistake, I don't think I want to..."

The rest of her sentence lost in the engine's fight roar.

Brad had no interest in her comments.

Outside the plane, Jack was enthusiastically waving goodbye.

Shelby fell back against the seat. With her emotions reeling, she was too frightened to speak.

Brad was given an all clear from the air traffic controller.

The Skyhawk's engine wound tightly sounding more like a model airplane than a functional aircraft.

There was nothing to fear, Shelby thought, the little engine could not possibly lift this airplane fifty feet off the ground much less them get them airborne.

Brad pushed forward on the steering column and the Cessna moved steadily forward. Brad grinned.

Shelby had seen that look before on the face of an infamous Hollywood boogieman right before he murdered the heroine.

For a moment everything seemed surreal, Shelby wondered if this was the first phase of an out-of-body experience.

Before she could say, "get me off this plane," the Cessna began its forward movement down the grassy runway.

No, no, no, Shelby screamed silently as the aircraft raced toward the end of the runway, passing anchored planes and small buildings too quickly.

With a dreadful whine she felt the plane rise a few feet off the ground, then higher and higher until it at last rose deftly over the tops of buildings and houses, climbing high into the blue cloudless Carolina sky.

I am going to faint, she thought, and was momentarily pleased. This is a good thing. If I die, I won't see it coming.

Gripping the side of her seat, she was unable to breathe. Her knuckles were white from the stain and yet seeing Hendersonville for the first time from the air was fascinating. Forgetting for just a moment the altitude, the tightness of the cockpit, her companion, and fear of flying, she was mesmerized by the landscape below her. She was able to recognize landmarks, buildings, and the mountains that surrounded this beautiful western Carolina hamlet. Shelby forgot everything but the incredible view.

Brad banked the plane to the left half then circled and headed east in a straight line toward Chimney Rock and Lake Lure.

"All right, Ms. Lake," Brad said, bringing both hands behind his head. "You can take over the plane now."

"What?" Shelby cried in alarm. She stared at the console with gears, knobs, and gadgets, then looked back to Brad. "What do you mean take over the plane? Are you insane?"

Brad chuckled.

"Fly the plane, Ms Lake," Brad repeated, his eyes narrowing, the tone of his voice dropping to a threatening growl. The little Cessna purred on heading east toward Hickory Nut Gorge.

"Take the controls! " Shelby shrieked. "Brad, take control!"

Brad sat perfectly calm, his hand resting comfortably at the back of his head.

"Seems like I remember reading somewhere Silver Lake is an accomplished pilot," Brad drawled with a slight glance at his watch. Turning back to her, he smiled, "Seeing how you are an accomplished pilot, I thought you'd enjoy flying the plane. Now take the controls before we crash."

"I can't fly this plane!" Shelby shrieked, unable to keep the panic out of her voice. Her breath quickened, her palms sweaty, and her cheeks burned with terror.

"You're Silver Lake, accomplished pilot, romance novelist and renowned Louisiana Chef."

"No, I'm not!" Shelby screamed in panic, "I'm not Silver Lake!"

To her astonishment, he showed no surprise.

With a private chuckle, Brad took control of the wheel.

"I know," he said, his voice cold and exact. "I know because I'm Silver Lake."

Breath caught in her lungs. "What?"

Below her the clear blue waters of Lake Lure sparkled in the midday sun and she caught sight of the oversized American Flag flying high over Chimney Rock Park.

She stared wordlessly at this big burly man who had just confessed to being one of America's most beloved romance novelists.

His eyes darkened for a moment as he held her gaze. Brad grinned enjoying the look on her face, but the game was up as he turned the plane back toward Hendersonville.

In a voice that demanded honesty, he asked, "But the question is, young lady, who are you? And what do you want with the Colters? They are dear friends of mine."

"I'm a private investigator," Shelby said, fumbling for a business card, "Maggie hired me to keep eye on Jack."

Brad stared out of window. "Why?"

"I don't know. She thinks someone is following Jack."

"Why did you choose the name Silver Lake?"

"It wasn't my idea," Shelby confessed. "It was Maggie's. Maggie wanted to keep my identity a secret from Jack. I don't know why and I don't know why she chose Silver Lake of all people."

Brad looked at her, his face void of expression. For several quiet moments she wasn't sure if he believed her or not.

"Look, I have identification on me," she tried to explain, but before she could reach for a business card, Brad's sudden roar of laugher filled the cockpit. It did little to relieve her anxiety.

Struggling to maintain his composure, his belly laugh filled the cockpit. "Why can't I write stuff like this?"

Shelby was stunned, his words at least registered with her. "You mean you really are the real Silver Lake?"

"Yes, I'm Silver Lake. I began writing novels about nine years ago. My agent and my publisher both suggested I write under a female pen name. We choose the name of Silver Lake and until this moment have successfully hidden behind the cover of my book. Only my publisher and agent know the truth. Ha! I was the one who introduced Maggie to my books."

Brad wiped a final tear of laughter from the corner of his eyes. "Now Miss, whatever your name is, private eye, for the moment, we will keep this our secret."

Shelby gave him a quick nod, grateful he wasn't going to throw her out of the plane, at least not yet. Gratefully she extended her hand across the cockpit and he grasped it in a warm handshake.

Shelby looked at the man and almost grinned.

"Nice to meet you Brad," Shelby said, "I'm Shelby MacGregor."

"That Maggie, what a corker!" Brad said, releasing her hand. "Sounds like something she would dream up to cover her tracks, but tell me, are the Colters really in trouble?"

"I'm not sure. Some suspicious characters have been seen in the neighborhood. The police are running IDs on them now. And you know that Jack's house was broken into last night."

"Jack seems convinced it was a couple of teenagers."

Brad nodded. "What do you think?"

"I think there's more to this," Shelby said honestly, "and I strongly suspect Maggie is hiding something from me. At any rate the truth will come out this afternoon when we intend on telling Jack the truth. This ruse has gone on long enough."

Brad let out a low whistle. "How do you two intend on telling Jack? Two things he hates in life, liars and these little escapades his mother is forever putting him in the middle of. If you like, I'll just happen to stop by. You may need a referee."

Shelby tried to smile. "That doesn't sound comforting, Brad."

"One more thing young lady, I have seen the sparks fly between you two. Don't think all his anger will be focused on just Maggie."

"I can't concern myself with Jack's feelings," Shelby lied, sounding very professional and polished, "he has to know the truth."

Shelby stared out the window and tried not to think of Jack's anger. Whether their relationship will be salvageable or not was not her primary concern at the moment, keeping Jack safe was.

High above Hendersonville, the minutes were slipping by quickly. Brad circled the runway twice waiting for another small plane to take off.

To keep from dying of a heart attack during the landing, Shelby was careful to keep her eyes closed. She took a small measure of comfort from knowing that if they crashed, she would at least be excused from facing Jack with the truth.

Luck however was against her, as Brad brought the little Skyhawk to a very smooth and uneventful landing.

Taxing to his apparent space, he brought the Cessna to a full stop and began flipping switches until the engine was completely shut down.

Busy with the switches and gauges, he didn't look at Shelby as he said, "I didn't mind so much your taking credits for my novels, but it really pissed me off when you took credit for my recipes."

"Wasn't me," Shelby protested. "Maggie whipped up dinner when I was out tailing Jack. I don't know why she felt compelled make that up."

There was a soft sparkle in Brad's eyes when he looked curiously at her. "Ms. MacGregor, are you a single?"

"Yes, why?" Shelby answered, puzzled by his odd question. "And call me Shelby."

Brad chuckled. "I wish Maggie was as interested in her own love life as she is in Jack's. Darn stubborn woman."

The last comment was spoken such affection, Shelby saw what she should have seen from the moment she had met him. Brad was in love with Maggie Colter. His concern about her had stemmed from his affection for her and Jack.

"Well, here comes your beau now," Brad said, pointing to Jack hurrying toward the plane.

Shelby grimaced watching him approach. A look of pure pleasure softened his handsome granite-like face. Time was no longer her friend but her enemy.

"I missed you," Jack said, opening the door of the Cessna. He nodded toward Brad and asked, "So how was the flight?"

"Informative," Shelby replied with a sideways glance to Brad.

Brad returned her smile.

"Ms. Lake, this was a real pleasure," Brad said returning her smile. "If I can be of further service, let me know."

"Later, Brad," Jack said, helping Shelby out of the plane. "And thanks for showing Silver the sights."

With a glance at Brad, Shelby waved goodbye. Intuitively she knew she had won a good friend and ally.

Jack's eyes were glowing with pleasure as she quickly told him how much she enjoyed the excursion. She omitted the part though about how she would never set foot in a small plane again.

Shelby's cell rang the moment she entered the Bronco moments later. It was Chris.

"Yes," she answered.

"Well, we know who our perpetrators are. A couple of small town hoods from South Carolina."

"Oh?" Shelby replied, hoping he would volunteer more.

Jack drove the Bronco out of the parking lot and toward downtown Hendersonville.

"Yeah, two idiots named Vernon and Maury Sims," Chris said. Shelby waited impatiently for him to continue.

Chris obliged with details. "They have been in and out of trouble all their lives.

For the most part petty stuff so far, they were serving time for a convenience store robbery when they escaped from a prison farm about six week ago."

With a glance toward Jack, Shelby said into the cell, "With all do respect, that sounds pretty serious to me."

Chris began to laugh.

"Wait till you hear this one," he said quickly, "they tried to rob a small convenience store in Florence, South Carolina. When they couldn't get the safe open, one of them had the brilliant idea to drag it home. So, they tied the safe to the bumper. When they heard the sirens, they drove away, only the safe pulled off the bumper with their license plate. The police were waiting for them by the time they arrived home. They escaped about five weeks ago. We have an all points bulletin about them now. It won't be long before they will be returned to South Carolina."

"Anything more?" Shelby asked, dreading Chris' answer.

"Not really, we don't know why they ended up here. Our bad luck maybe. We checked, they have no known friends or relatives here."

"All right," Shelby said, hoping Chris would understand her next comments, "I need about an hour. Could you get back with me, with us then?"

"Got ya," Chris replied, "I guess your undercover assignment will be over soon."

"Exactly," Shelby answered, signing off.

"You look worried, "Jack said, his brow wrinkled, "not bad news with one of your books?"

Shelby gave him a half nod. He reached out and gently cupped her hand.

She was grateful for the small comfort of his touch. Jack would know the truth about her in a matter of minutes

Passing the Western Carolina Community Bank, Shelby noticed a late model burgundy Saturn oddly parked in the parking lot. The driver's door was open but no driver was in sight.

She sat up. "Jack, that looks like your mother's car."

Hitting the brakes hard, Jack made a sharp turn into the parking lot, ignoring the loud honk behind him. He pulled up behind the sedan. "It's my mother's car, alright; I can't imagine why she'd leave the door open."

Both Shelby and Jack jumped from the vehicle.

"Mother!" Jack shouted, seeing the Saturn empty. He looked back at Shelby. "Where the heck is she? Why would she have left the door open?"

He started to reach toward the door, but Shelby shot her arm before him, forcibly stopping him from moving closer to the car.

"Don't touch anything," Shelby warned. "Look there."

Jack looked at her and followed her line of vision to an envelope secured to the windshield wiper.

Shelby reached in her purse pulled out a small pair of plastic gloves she kept for emergencies. Slipping them on, she reached for the note.

"What does it say?" Jack demanded his voice impatient.

Shelby felt the hit to her stomach as she read, "Don't call the cops. We will get in touch with you. We got Maggie Colter. We want money, lots of it."

Gently laying the note atop the car, she secured it under the windshield wiper blade. She grabbed her cell and hit 9-1-1.

"What are you doing!" Jack shouted at her. "It says not to call the police!"

"Jack, we have no choice!" Shelby explained as the dispatcher answered. "Your Mother has been kidnapped!"

CHAPTER EIGHT

The note says not to call the police!"

Shelby steadied her gaze. She had to make him understand. In a voice that held lethal calmness, she softly articulated each word. "Jack, it's very important that we call the police immediately. Trust me, please, just trust me in this."

For several long seconds he stared at her. His eyes were dark with worry. Helpless he reached for Maggie's purse but Shelby reached out and took a firm grip upon his wrist before he could touch the handbag.

"Don't touch anything," she warned then explained delicately, "there may be fingerprints or other clues as to Maggie's whereabouts or who took her. I can't let you touch anything."

Jack stood helplessly staring at Maggie's car. Shelby had no time to comfort him. Pulling her cell out of her pocket, she punched in 9-1-1.

Jack stood looking lost, helpless, angry, and enraged.

Shelby turned away from him and said quickly, "There's been a kidnapping at the Western Carolina Community at Main and Magnolia. The victim's name is Maggie Colter. She is 5'6", approximately 160 lbs, gray hair, last seen wearing," she stopped, oh what had Maggie been wearing that morning. Her trained recall went into overdrive. "She was last scene wearing a pink blouse, short sleeved, and a pair of beige slacks. Suspects may be two white men seen in a 1995 brown Ford pickup with South Carolina license plates."

"Officers are being directed to the scene," the dispatcher answered briskly.

It seemed only moments before two Hendersonville squad cars came screeching into the parking lot.

Chris was in the second car.

Both officers hurried to the Saturn. Shelby held up the note for Chris to read.

"Chief's on his way," Chris said to Jack and Shelby. He held out his hand to Jack.

"I'm Officer Chris Turner. We met the other night, Mr. Colter."

"Yes," Jack answered, grasping Chris' hand for a short greeting.

"What do we do now?"

"This is Officer Mike Howell, Mr. Colter," Chris continued, "he's going to secure the scene. I think it best if we return to your mother's house. They said they would get in touch with us. We need to go to the house and wait for the call."

Jack nodded. His face turned ashen as he watched Officer Mike Howell begin to use bright yellow crime scene tape to partition around the parameter of Maggie's car.

"We need to go, Jack," Shelby said, softly touching his sleeve, "the police will contact us if anything more is found. We need to go to your mother's house. We need to wait for the call."

"All right," Jack said, his voice sounding stained, "let's go."

"Are you coming with us?" Shelby asked Chris. He gave her a nod and hurried back to his squad car.

In a matter of minutes, Jack and Shelby were back in the Bronco and Chris was following behind.

"Which house?" Jack cried. "The note said they would call us. My mother's house or mine?"

Shelby stared at him. He was right. The note didn't specify which house the ransom call would come into. She took a breath, calculating the next critical moments.

"Go to yours. I'll wait at Maggie's. Both will be covered."

Jack gripped the wheel of the Bronco intent on reaching the houses. The momentary confusion and helplessness was giving way to a direct course of action. He needed something to 'do' to protect his mother. Understanding this, Shelby watched as Jack's demeanor changed from one of helplessness to an outraged son who would see his mother home this day.

Shelby, softly reaching across the seat for his hand said, "It'll be all right. We will get Maggie back safely, I promise."

As he turned to her, she saw the doubt in his eyes, but he managed a half smile as he accepted the comfort of her small hand.

By the time they reached the Colter homes, their course was set. Wasting no time, Jack pulled into his driveway.

Shelby was out of the Bronco before Jack made a full stop.

"The door is probably unlocked," he shouted out to her as she crossed the distance to Maggie's house.

Shelby heard the phone ringing before she reached the steps.

"The phone!" she screamed to Jack, jerking Maggie's back door open.

Don't stop ringing, she screamed silently as she crossed the kitchen floor.

"Hello?" she breathlessly cried into the receiver.

"Who is this?" a wiry voice demanded from the other end.

Shelby tried to sound casual but she was out of breath.

"I'm a house guest of Maggie Colter. She isn't home right now; can I take your number and tell her you called?"

"You are that writer lady?" the voice whined in a strong southern accent, "Maggie told us all about you. Said you were staying at her house."

"Yes," Shelby said, trying to sound calm. As Jack bolted into the kitchen she said firmly, "I'm Silver Lake, how can I help you?"

"Well, we've got Maggie Colter. You tell that boy of hers that we want some money."

"Is this a crank call?" Shelby asked, trying to sound calmer than she felt. "Who are you?"

"Never mind that, you ain't gonna trick me," the voice on the other end of the line snarled. He cleared his throat and spoke as clearly as someone like him could.

"It don't matter who I am Ms. Fancy Pants Writer Woman. What is important is we kidnapped Maggie Colter."

"Is she all right?" Shelby snapped, "I have to know if she is all right?"

"She's just fine," the voice assured her. "Now I want you to get a pen and paper."

"Okay," Shelby said, looking to Jack, she made a charade movement to scribbling pen to paper.

"I'm looking now for a piece of paper," she assured the caller. Jack pulled open several drawers before he found a notepad and a pen. He handed them to Shelby as Chris Turner entered the room.

Looking directly at Chris she once again pantomimed she had the kidnapers on the other phone. Chris nodded and went out the back door.

Shelby knew he was going to attempt a trace of the call. She had to keep the kidnapper on the phone as long as possible.

"Okay, okay. I have the paper and pen you wanted me get."

Shelby heard a chuckle at the other end.

"I want you to make a list," the voice said.

Taking time to answer she replied, "I'm ready. I'll write down your list, but first I want to be sure Maggie is all right. I need to talk to her."

The caller put his hand over the phone. She could barely hear the muffled sounds of the caller's explanation and argument to another second person in the room.

"No. You ain't gonna talk to her."

"Put her on," Shelby argued.

This time there was no attempt to cover the open argument that followed.

"What does she want now?" she heard a second male voice drawl impatiently.

"She wants to talk to Maggie Colter," the caller explained, sounding exasperated.

"Just a dat burn minute," the caller said to Shelby.

Shelby listened to several more impassioned pleas before the second voice relented.

"All right, you can talk to her," the caller said, not sounding too happy.

A scuffle of sounds was heard as if the phone were taken from one room to another. Shelby strained for anything that would identify the location. She heard the muffled orders and suddenly, gratefully, she heard Maggie's voice.

"Silver dear, it's me, Maggie."

Shelby motioned to Jack; his mother was one the line.

"Are you all right?" Shelby asked of Maggie.

"Yes, I'm fine dear. I'm out by..."

"That's enough!" the caller shouted and was once again on the line. "You rich people think you're so clever. Well, you ain't! We're the smart ones. You're the dumb ones."

"All right then," Shelby said, hardly satisfied, "what is it you want?"

"I gotta list right here," the caller said, pride resonating in his voice.

Shelby heard the shuffle of papers.

"We want," he said as if beginning to read from a script, "$ 50,000."

"OK, you want $ 50,000," Shelby repeated.

"What? What? Hey, hold on," the caller told her. In muffled tones he was speaking to the second man in the room.

"Change that little lady," he said, coming back onto the line. "Make that

$ 100,000, yeah, $ 50,000 a piece. And we want it in small, unmarked bills."

"$100,000," Shelby repeated. "Is that all?"

"Tell him yes!" Jack spat, his face twisting in anguish.

"That's a lot of money," Shelby said, slowly shaking her head at Jack. With her index finger high in the air she tried to show him she was stalling for time. To the kidnapper she added, "We don't just have that kind of money lying around. It's going to take us time to get that money together."

"The Colters are rich," the man argued, "shouldn't take that long a'all."

"You'll have to give me time," Shelby said, stalling. Chris opened the screen door and pinched his hands together and drew them out. Shelby knew he wanted to keep the men on the phone. Shelby nodded in understanding.

Chris closed the door as quietly as he had opened it.

"Is there anything else you want?" Shelby asked, trying to come up with more conversation to keep them on the line.

There was a long pause.

Shelby listened as the caller asked his partner if there was more they wanted.

"Well, I don't know," the kidnapper replied to his companion, "you think of something?"

"Since you asked," the caller said smartly, "you ken bring us some clothes from the store."

"What store?" Shelby asked, knowing full well they meant Bear Creek Outfitters, the Colter's store.

She glanced at her watch. Chris should have gotten the trace by now.

"Well, for Pete's sake, the Colter store!" the caller snapped. "You ain't that smart for a writer after all, is you?"

"Okay," Shelby agreed, and then asked, "what kind of clothes?"

"She wants to know what kind of clothes, Maury?"

Maury, one was named Maury. Maury Sims, she thought with satisfaction. The other voice had to be Vernon Sims. These were the escapees from South Carolina. The ones who were driving the stolen brown truck.

"Okay, we want some shirts," the caller demanded. "The shirts need to be a size large and medium."

"You want shirts?" she repeated, not quite believing they had asked for clothing.

"Yeah," the voice said with as much authority as he could manage, "large and medium."

"What about pants?" Shelby asked, realizing they had not a clue the call was being traced. They had obviously not read kidnapping for dummies.

"Oh yeah, the pants, size 36 for me. What size you wear Vern?"

"What size?" the caller demanded impatiently." I don't know what size, look at the back of your britches."

A short pause was followed by a muffled voice in the background.

Maury came back on the phone. "Okay, size 34 and size 36, got that?"

Chris came into the kitchen and held up his thumb. The grin on his face told her the call was being traced. She would only need a couple more minutes.

"Anything else?" Shelby asked impulsively. Thinking no one would be this stupid, she suggested, "You know they got a lot of nice stuff at the store downtown. How about a pair of hiking boots?"

"Yeah!" the caller almost cheered, "two pair of those fancy hiking boots."

"Got it," Shelby said slowly. "Anything else? You boys like to go fishing? I bet they have more equipment down there than they need."

"Yeah, good thinking," the caller said brightly. "Bring us some of those fishing poles. The nice ones."

"Wow, you boys are going to make a nice haul out of this," Shelby said with a glance at her watch. Then with as much false admiration she could muster, she said, "Now you know it will take us a little time to gather all that together."

"Well, reckon you better hop on it. We'll give you a holler back in an hour."

"Where do we take this stuff?" Shelby asked.

"She wants to know where to do the drop off everything," the man said to his companion in a whisper. Apparently the kidnapping was not that well planned out.

"Well, I don't know," she caught another exchange of whispers.

"We're gonna call back in an hour. You just hurry on up and get that stuff together."

"Look, I'll have to go to the bank. I have to go to the store. I'll need more time than that. You'll have to give me more time."

"We'll call back in one hour, and remember the fishing poles."

With the last request spoken the line went dead.

"Did you get the trace?"

"What's going on?" Brad McClannahan demanded, coming into the back door. "I heard all the commotion on the police scanner."

Brad nodded his head toward Chris but looked to Shelby who was just placing the phone back on the receiver.

"My mother has been kidnapped," Jack explained quickly.

Brad's mouth dropped open. "You've got to be kidding!"

"We've got the trace," Chris interjected triumphantly. "They're out just off Highway 64, toward Holmes Forest. I want you to wait here for their call. I'm going out there now."

"We're going too," Shelby said, grabbing her purse.

"No," Chris said, motioning toward the phone. "You need to wait for the next call. The Chief's on his way there along with the Sheriff's Department. To be on the safe side, if you have the money, you might want to get it together. I'm going to go out that way and see if I can locate the house."

Without further ado, Chris left. Minutes later, they heard the sounds of his police care peeling out of the driveway.

"This is a nightmare," Jack said, raking his fingers through his hair.

"The officer's right," Brad said, his face ashen. "Let's get what we can together for Maggie. What can I do to help?"

Jack looked at the list.

"They want $ 100,000 and some things at the store."

"I can get whatever you need from the store," Brad said, not bothering to hide the pain in his eyes.

Jack gave him a quick smile. "I'll call the store manager and make sure he has the clothes, fishing poles, and whatever else they else wanted ready for you to pick up. I'll tell him to gather whatever cash we have on hand. I'll have a check made out to you for $100,000."

Brad almost jerked the list from Jack's hand and hurried out the way he came.

Leaving Jack to call in to the store, Shelby raced upstairs. She grabbed her glock to make sure it was fully loaded. Finding her ankle holster, she slid the gun safely into it before dropping two full clips into her purse.

"I called the store," Jack said, his brow taunt with uneasiness. "Our manager is getting everything together now."

Helpless to do more, he paced across the kitchen floor.

"What are we supposed to do now?"

The phone rang.

"You better answer," Jack said with a worried glance toward the phone. "I'm not sure I can keep my temper in check with these two goons."

"Silver Lake," Shelby said into the receiver.

"Bring the money to the maintenance shed at Holmes Forest," Maury Sims instructed her.

"I don't know where that is," Shelby said, stalling for time.

"Well, then, you'd best just figure it out. First go to Holmes Forest, then go to the parking lot, you'll see a phone there by the restrooms; wait there and we'll tell you where to drop off our stuff."

"What about Maggie?" Shelby demanded.

"When we get our stuff, you get Mrs. Colter."

"We are getting everything together now," Shelby told the caller.

"Well, you have got two hours, Ms. Lake," the voice said smartly. "Get everything we asked for then or poor old Mrs. Colter will be history."

"We are getting everything together right now," Shelby repeated, but the caller had already ended the call.

She slowly returned the phone to its cradle and looked at Jack.

"They want us to take the money to the maintenance shed at Holmes Forest. It has to be there in two hours."

Jack glanced at his watch. He took a deep breath. "We should have everything together by then. It sure doesn't leave us much time."

"Jack," Shelby said, going to his side.

He pulled her body in for comfort and held her tightly.

"I should have taken that break-in more seriously," he said, his voice dripping with guilt.

"It's not your fault," Shelby said, her voice cracking with guilt. "And there's something I need to tell you."

Shelby stopped as she caught gaze of the small prescription bottle next to the sink. With a sharp intake of breath, she pointed at it. "Jack! Is that your mother's medicine? How often is she supposed to take it?"

"It's her medicine, she must have forgotten it," Jack said, his face ashen. "She should have had it two hours ago. She must have been returning home to get it when they abducted her."

Shelby grabbed the small brown container and held it tightly.

"How long can she go without her medicine?" Shelby asked, seeing the stricken look on Jack's face.

"She takes a tablet at lunch," Jack said, staring at the bottle and then at his watch. "She must have left her medicine here this morning. That's why she was on here way home. Silver, she should have taken this about two hours ago!"

"Look," Shelby said, "I'm going after Chris. You wait here in case they call back."

"You are not leaving without me! We'll go together!"

Though she knew better, she also knew she didn't have a chance to leave without him.

"We'll both go then," Shelby said, slipping Maggie's medicine into her purse.

"What if they call?" Jack said, glancing toward the phone.

Shelby looked at the white cordless telephone.

"Does your mother have call forwarding?"

For a moment Jack looked confused, then his eyes brightened. "Yes, she does. I bet her pass code is the same she uses at work."

With a short exhale, she said, "Forward the calls to your cell phone, the kidnappers will never know the difference."

With that, she left the house.

Jack's Bronco was parked behind his house. Wasting no time, Shelby pulled her keys out and hurried toward her little Chevy Tracker.

"Let s take the Tracker," she called out to him when he emerged from the house moments later.

"We need to get the ransom money and the things from the store," Jack reminded her.

Unlocking the doors to the Tracker, they both climbed in.

"Call the store and let Brad know what is going on."

Starting the engine, she immediately shifted gears, throwing the little SUV into reverse.

"Jack, there's something I've been wanting to tell you for days," she began, already sensing how badly all this was going to come out.

"Silver honey, I'm not worried about anything you have to tell me," Jack assured her. "And I am not sure if I can exactly stand any bad news at the moment. I'm just grateful you are with me. I thank God for your cool head."

She hardly glanced at him as she wheeled the Tracker into the street. She shoved the gear back to first and forced the gas pedal to the floor. Rapidly shifting the gears she matched the engine's whine to the forced acceleration.

Zigzagging through neighborhood streets, she took little-known shortcuts that only a local would know. Jack was too distraught to notice her familiarity with Hendersonville's streets.

Quickly, she took them to the outskirts of town and onto Highway 64.

"Do you have any idea where we are going?" Jack asked over the rush of speed.

"Somewhere out by Holmes Forest. The police car can't be too far ahead of us," Shelby replied breathlessly, downshifting to pass several vehicles.

With the road clear before her, she forced the Tracker to a breakneck speed. Jack didn't protest his eyes on the road before him.

Ignoring the 45 mile an hour speed limit through Etowah, she honked the horn warning a driver from pulling out in front of her.

Out of Etowah, Shelby once again forced the Tracker to accelerate rapidly.

The road open before them, she kept a firm grasp of the wheel, smoothly taking the sharp turns and increasing her speed down straight-aways. They reached the turn to Holmes Education Forest and made a hard turn.

Chris had to have turned off the main road, she thought. Trusting her instincts, she turned down the first secondary road.

A quarter of a mile down the road, she miraculously spotted the distinct blue lights of a patrol car ahead of her. Chris had his lights on but not the siren. She closed the distance between them.

The patrol car almost lifted as it crossed a small bridge. Keeping plenty of breaking distance between them, she followed as close as she could.

About a mile and a half down the road, Chris turned off the flashers and slowed. He overshot a single driveway and parked the squad car behind a patch of overgrown bushes planted along the road.

Seeing him slow, Shelby brought the Tracker to a halt in front of a long drive. The Tracker was safely hidden behind a mailbox and some shrubs.

Down the long overgrown drive she could see a white frame farmhouse surrounded by abandoned vehicles and unused farm equipment.

"Is my mother here?" Jack asked his voice was filled with strain. He looked down the long drive to the decrepit old abandoned farmhouse.

"I think so," Shelby answered, looking behind her. Chris had no back up at the moment. No back up but her.

"Now what," Jack said, grabbing the door handle.

"Now we wait," Shelby said, trying to steady her voice. She watched Chris get out of the patrol car. He looked at her direction and pointed toward the

farmhouse.

With visual contact, she waved her hand telling him she had his back. Just like old times, she thought with a smile.

"Jack, let's get out of the Tracker," she said softly, and added, "quietly."

Though they were a goodly distance from the farmhouse, Shelby did not want to take a chance of alerting the kidnappers.

Chickens were roaming freely in the front yard of the farmhouse squawked in warning, but no one came from the house.

Jack made his way around the Tracker.

"Now what do we do," he asked her in hushed tones.

"At this moment, I'm sure; police officers from three counties are on their way here right now. We need to wait," Shelby said, keeping her eyes on the farmhouse.

Quickly she scanned the drive, the barn, and the house, looking for advantage points, and praying the hostage negotiator would arrive with the next police car.

"There must be something we can do," Jack said, his eyes never once leaving the farmhouse.

Shelby shook her head. "Not without putting your mother's life in more danger than it is. We have to wait for more law enforcement to arrive."

At that moment, Jack's cell rang, and he looked at Shelby.

"You better take this. It might be the kidnappers and they will be thinking we are at my mother's house."

Shelby accepted the phone and pressed the talk receiver.

"Hello," she said, trying to keep any trace of anxiety from her voice.

"It's me," the caller identified himself. "Have you got the money?"

"We're working on it," Shelby replied.

She could see the look of anxiety in Jack's eyes, but could do little to console him. Gratefully, the men were also buying into the fact she was at Maggie's house and not standing 150 yards from where they were calling.

"Well, work faster," the voice told her in angry tones. "Now we're gonna call you back in twenty minutes. You better got the money and stuff we want, Ms. Lake."

Feeling the perspiration on her forehead she asked, "Is Maggie Colter all right?"

"She is just fine and dandy," the caller assured her. "I'll call you back. Make sure you have all the money then."

The line went dead. Shelby passed the phone back to Jack.

"They are going to call us back in about twenty minutes. They must be going to put some kind of plan into action. We need to stay alert and pray more law enforcement officers arrive soon."

At that moment, the screen door opened. A man Shelby recognized as the man who had pumped the gas into the Ford pickup came out. She glanced at Chris who had drawn his revolver and was pointed directly at the suspect.

"Why doesn't he just shoot?" Jack demanded.

Chris did have a clean shot but it was too risky. She knew he wouldn't take the chance of endangering Maggie.

"He can't," Shelby said to Jack. Looking back to the farmhouse, she saw the screen door open a second time and heard Jack's sharp intake of breath as they watched Maggie walk out onto the porch.

Though her hair was slightly out of place, and she looked a bit shaken, she stopped, as though to adjust her eyes toward the sunlight.

Shelby felt her heart sink realizing Maggie did not have on a blindfold on, hoping it was because the men were too stupid to realize Maggie would be able to later identify them, she held her gaze steady on the older woman. She was clearly agitated but she was unharmed.

The second man emerged and for some reason took great care locking the door on the house. Shelby looked at Chris. He shook his head.

She nodded in agreement. This was no good. The kidnappers were bound to see her car or the patrol car in a matter of moments.

Shelby looked back to the farmhouse to see the two men escorting Maggie away from house toward the brown pickup truck parked near the barn.

Shelby felt Jack tense beside her. "What are they doing?"

"They are moving her. Maybe taking her with them to pick up their ransom; what boneheads!" Shelby hissed, "why couldn't they have left Maggie in the farmhouse until the ransom was secure?"

Across the distance, she saw Chris looking at her. He also knew taking Maggie with them was not safe. Shelby knew Chris would have to intervene.

Chris readied his revolver and jumped the ditch.

With his arms fully extended, the revolver pointed directly at the men, he moved closer toward them.

"I'm Officer Chris Turner with the Hendersonville Police Department," he shouted out to the men. "Drop your weapons. You're under arrest."

They stopped and seemed momentarily stunned to find a fully armed law enforcement officer approaching them.

Chris continued to move forward, keeping his gun steady.

"I want you boys to drop your guns, and lay down on the ground. Do it now!"

"What are we gonna do, Maury?" The younger, scruffier man said to his older companion.

"Stay right there for a minute," Maury called out to Chris. "Don't come any closer or we will shoot the woman."

"Maury," the younger explained, "if we shoot the woman, we don't get the money."

"Shut up, Vern."

"I don't guess you boys heard me," Chris warned them, drawing closer. "I want you to put your firearms on the ground and lay down. Hands on your head. Mrs. Colter, move away from the men."

"He ain't a gonna shoot us," Maury said with a sneer. He pulled Maggie closer to him and brandished a pistol. "He ain't a gonna risk killing the Colter woman."

With that, Maury raised the gun and pointed it at Chris. He fired as Chris dove behind a small brick well in the yard. Maury took two more shots at Chris.

The second blast hit and exploded into the well's side, causing a thick shower of dust and small rocks to explode beside him.

He was pinned down.

Maggie was in danger.

Reaching down, Shelby lifted her pants leg and unsnapped the ankle holster. In one fluid movement, she had the glock nestled deep in her hand.

A quick snap of the safety, she moved toward the end of the SUV intent on sliding down the side of the driveway, drawing fire away from Chris.

"What the hell are you doing?" Jack said, watching both his mother, the men, and Chris who was pinned down behind the well. The kidnapers fired off two more rounds.

"I'm going to save your mother!" Shelby snapped. She began moving away from the Tracker, following down the driveway.

"But you are a romance novelist!" she heard Jack scream behind her.

CHAPTER NINE

In a half crouch, both hands firmly around the glock, Shelby moved quickly toward the farmhouse. The drive was grassy and narrow. Through she felt exposed in open view; she knew she was hidden from view behind trees, bushes, and piles of trash that separated her from the men.

The men had stopped firing. They stood as if not stood not sure what to do next. Maggie stood shaking next to the taller of the two.

Behind her, Jack was helpless but to watch the unfolding drama.

With the men's attention solely upon Chris, Shelby moved quickly and quietly down the drive. As she inched her way up behind the back of the truck, their voices were more distinct, their words clearer.

She looked down the drive.

The men stood twelve yards away from her unkempt, with shabby overalls and faded shirts, and their hair long out of fashion. They stood arguing, their voices loud, strained, and heavy with uneducated southern accents.

Shelby crouched behind the tailgate. She had a second to decide her next move.

"Now look what you've done. Maury! When they catch us we're gonna be in big fat trouble. So, Mr. Smarty, what we gonna do now?"

Maury wiped his brow toward the younger man. "Who says we are gonna get caught, fool? In about twenty minutes, we're gonna be rich. 'Sides, what was I supposed to do? That policeman was gonna ruin our plan, Vern."

Shelby rose slowly from behind the truck. Too absorbed in their own argument they were totally unaware of her. Small advantage.

As if feeling her presence, Maggie turned almost in slow motion and looked straight at her. Her eyes lit, and her mouth curled slowly into a sweet smile.

Shelby motioned with too quick a tilt of her head for Maggie to move away from the men, and toward the opposite side of the truck.

"We are gonna be rich," Maury repeated in a sing song voice.

Vern frowned and looked back toward the well. "But what about that cop? He ain't going to let us just drive out of here. We gotta do something with him."

"Vernon, you are the dumbest cluck I have ever seen. No, we can't shoot him. When they catch us and he's dead, they might fry us."

Vernon mouthed the word 'oh.'

Maggie continued to move slowly to the side of the truck

"Hey, Mr. Police Man, you stay right there. Hear?" Maury shouted toward Chris. "We're gonna drive out of here. If you follow us, I'm gonna shoot, got that Vern?"

Maggie was now on the opposite side of the truck. Shelby, with both hands on the glock ,raised it in front of her.

"What did you say?" Vernon asked angrily, turning toward Maury. "If the cop follows, you are gonna shoot me? What kind of a fool plan is that?"

"No, I ain't gonna shoot you," Maury explained. "I said if the cop follows us, I was gonna shoot."

"Who?"

"Who do you think?" Maury shouted at Vern, "I'm gonna shoot at the cop."

"Oh," Vernon said, at last understanding Maury, but suspiciously eyeing his companion.

Vernon stood several moments. He brought his hand to his face and pointed two fingers at his eyes then shot them back to Maury. Giving Maury the big eye he said aloud, "My eye is on you."

Maggie was now completely behind the truck.

Shelby motioned for Maggie to duck down behind the truck. Without hesitation, she did.

"Oh great! Miss Maggie is gone," Maury said with sudden anxiety. Looking around he asked of his co-conspirator, "Where'd she go?"

"How do I know? You were supposed to be watching her!" Vern ground out each word between his teeth. His fresh anger directed at Maury.

"Well, she had got to be 'round here somewhere," Maury countered, "she didn't vanish into thin air. You were supposed to be watching her too."

"Me?" Maury challenged him, "I was shooting at the cop. Do I have to do everything?"

"Mrs. Colter," Vernon called out again in a sing-song voice best reserved for gathering barnyard chickens.

With outstretched hands, Shelby raised the gun chest high and stepped out from the truck.

"Who the heck are you?" Vernon said, almost annoyed. He elbowed Maury who jumped in surprise to find Shelby standing yards away from with. Her gun pointed directly at his head.

Vernon raised his gun back toward Chris, then to Shelby, then back toward Chris.

"What?" he shouted, waving the gun about, "Is this a dang gone party? Did we send out invites? Who the heck is she?"

"Settle down," Shelby said in an even voice.

The glock was ready to fire. She couldn't help the stray thought that she would be doing the world a favor by shooting these two idiots before they had a chance to have children.

"Shoot her, Vern. Shoot her!" Maury shouted.

Shelby kept the gun steady.

Incredibly Vernon stood without movement. Shelby held the glock firmly, pointing directly at his head.

"Are you a cop?" he asked in a tone that was cool and suspicious.

"No, but I play one on TV," Shelby answered. Taking a step closer to the men, she knew she now dominated the moment. She was fully in the open. She had successfully drawn their attention away from the truck, away from Maggie.

"You ain't on TV," Vernon replied with a snort of laughter. "If you were on TV, I would recognize you. I guess I look dumb, ugh?"

Pointing the gun directly at Vernon, she didn't bother to answer him.

"Ask her if she is a cop," Maury urged him. "If she's a cop, she has to tell you."

"Hey, are you a cop?" Vernon said with his voice raised.

"Come to think of it," Maury interjected, "she only has to tell you that if she's a cop pretending to be a prostitute. I don't think she is prostitute."

"Oh," Vernon said with a nod. "Right, but I don't think she's a prostitute, I mean with the gun and all."

Down to her last nerve, Shelby said, "I'm a private

investigator. I've been trailing you for days. Now, lay your weapons on the ground and raise your hands over your head."

"She is lying," Maury called out, "I bet she is lying."

Shelby took a step closer to Vern. She adjusted her aim and kept her gun steady.

"Maury," Vernon said, shifting his stance, "she has got the gun right on me. What do I do?"

"Vernon put your gun down, NOW!" Shelby warned in a voice edged with steel.

"How do you know my name?"

Shelby almost smiled.

"Vernon," Shelby repeated slowly, evenly, her voice heavy in exasperation. "I'm a former law enforcement officer. The policeman you have pinned down over there is my partner. Now, I know how to use this gun and I will. This is your last warning. Put the gun down now!"

"Shoot her, shoot her," Maury called out.

"I don't know 'bout that, Maury," Vernon said slowly. His voice was beginning to rise. "She's pointing a gun at me. I ain't killed anyone before, besides I think if I fire, she'll shoot me dead. I'm plum certain of it."

"That is right, Vern," Shelby acknowledged. "I don't want to shoot you and you don't want to be dead. This is the last time I am going to tell you."

Shelby took another step forward, "You boys are in a lot of trouble. Let's not make it any worse. Drop the gun. This is your last warning!"

For a moment, Vernon stood motionless. A look of resignation flashed in his eyes. He was beaten. His shoulders and his body slumped. He raised the gun in his palm, finger off the trigger and slowly lowered it to the ground.

LINN RANDOM

As the gun dropped in slow motion to the grassy mound beside him, Shelby wiped her body toward Maury and with a steady hand said, "Game's over Maury. Drop your gun!"

"Oh man!" Maury cried, "I said this wasn't gonna work!! I said we should have gone on to Tennessee and robbed a bank. You and your big ideas!"

"Me?" Vernon challenged him, "I said we should go to Tennessee. Did you listen? Nooooo!"

Though he was lowering his gun, Shelby remained poised, anticipating a second gun from either man.

"Do as the lady says," Chris said, seemingly appearing out of thin air.

Shelby smiled slightly. Knowing he would, Chris had taken advantage of the moment to come undetected into the arena.

"You have got two guns pointed at you, Maury," Chris warned the kidnapper. "Drop the gun. Put your hands on your head."

With both guns upon him, he looked at Chris and Shelby before finally dropping his gun to his side. It fell to the soft thick grass. Maury raised his hands to his head. He obviously knew the routine well and seemed almost impatient for Chris to follow with the cuffs and his Miranda Rights.

"Cheer up, Mr. Sims, you will enjoy our prisons a whole lot better than the ones in South Carolina," Chris said, pulling his cuffs from his belt.

"Should have robbed that bank in Tennessee," Maury said under his breath, though loud enough for everyone to hear, "We'd been rich instead of going back to JAIL!"

Chris was upon Maury and kicked the gun away from him. Pulling down one arm behind his back, he snapped a cuff on his wrist before pulling down the second and securely cuffing the other. Shoving him to the ground, Chris threw a pair of cuffs at Shelby and grinned.

"Seems like old times, partner," he called out to her.

"Yeah, sure seems like old times, partner," she repeated. Chris turned his gun on Vernon and Shelby shoved the glock in her jeans. She quickly cuffed Vernon and shoved him toward the truck.

She kicked his feet apart and with both hands Shelby patted down his waist, down his legs, and back up again searching for a gun, a knife, any weapon he might have hidden.

Chris brought Maury up beside Vernon and shoved him down in front of the driver door.

"Sit there," Chris warned the men with a grin toward Shelby.

"Maggie!" Shelby called out, "It's over. Come out."

From behind the truck, Maggie emerged. Her blue eyes faint and uncertain as she looked to Shelby and Chris. Seeing her kidnappers cuffed and seated on the ground she took a slow step away from the truck.

"Maggie, they are cuffed. It's okay. You're safe," Shelby assured her.

Looking no worse for wear, Maggie came around the truck. Color was quickly returning to her face, along with a deep seated look of utter satisfaction.

With a slight nod of gratitude toward Shelby and Chris, she immediately went to her kidnappers.

"Shame, shame, shame," she said to their downward turned heads. "You two should not have kidnapped me. I told you so."

"Yes madam," they drawled in unison.

"And, you should have waited for back up," Shelby chided Chris. Her was body flooding with immense relief.

Chris grinned, "They were moving her. I had no choice. Besides, they would have seen the patrol car. I saw your Chevy up the road and I knew I had you as back up. Thanks."

Shelby looked back at Maggie but was hardly surprised to find her almost giddy with delight.

"This was all so exciting," Maggie squealed like a child, "wait 'til this gets around town!"

Maggie waved her finger at the men one more time, "I told you nothing good would come of this, young men. Now you are really in hot water."

"We're sorry," they repeated in unison, not daring to look at their victim.

"Maggie," Shelby said and softly held out her arms for a hug. Maggie gratefully accepted the comfort of Shelby's arms and pulled back. Her eyes shining, her smile wide and full.

"I knew you would come for me, dear," she said with calm assurance.

As Chris began to recite their Miranda Rights, Shelby saw Jack marching down the driveway.

His steps were deliberate, at the short step. Instead of relief, his face was dark with rage. His blue eyes were black with anger. His jaw pronounced. With his shoulders square, Jack's hands were clinched as if ready to attack. His warm full lips were taut, tight, and twisted in fury. All softness, all tenderness was gone. This was not the man she knew.

"Are you okay?" he asked his mother. But his eyes were cold upon Shelby. His eyes were contemptuous and filled with unspoken accusations.

Shelby stood before this cold stranger. She waited for understanding, compassion, gratitude, or even humanity. She found none.

"Oh yes," Maggie replied to her son. "I don't think I was in any real danger at all. These boys were harmless enough. Well, except for trying to kill that nice officer. Oh my goodness, what an adventure!"

Three police cars wheeled into the dirt drive followed by an orange and white rescue squad.

Maggie, no worse for wear, allowed Jack to gather her into his arms.

"See, I'm all right, there was no need to worry."

"I have got your pills," Shelby said, remembering the small valve in her pocket. She handed them to Maggie who quickly opened the valve.

"Thank you dear," Maggie said without ceremony, "didn't take one at noon."

Looking down at Shelby, Jack stood his entire 6'1" height. His face was now black with unbridled rage.

"Who are you?" he demanded, his voice hard and cold and resonated within her as though it was an echo from an empty tomb.

Before Shelby could speak, Maggie turned into Jack, protectively placing herself between her son and Shelby.

"She's the woman who saved my life," Maggie answered for Shelby. "And I will thank you to have the good manners to stop scowling at her."

"So," Jack said smartly to his mother, "you know who she is. Are you in on this too, Mom?"

"Don't use that tone with your mother," Shelby countered.

Crossing his arms, Jack stood, now glaring at both women.

"I take it you're not Silver Lake," he spat, "the romance novelist."

"No," Shelby answered. There was so much to tell him. How could she begin? How could she make him understand when all he saw were lies?

"Jack, I tried to tell you," Shelby stammered, searching the dark blue eyes for the man she had come to know. "I tried to tell you a dozen times."

"You didn't try hard enough," came his hot reply.

"Now don't you get your back up, Jackson Colter," Maggie scolded like a little banty hen protecting her young. Maggie's body stiffened and she waved a sharp finger at Jack.

"This was my idea, not hers," Maggie said, coming to her full stature. "And what was done was done to protect you."

Jack laughed and placed his hands on his hips.

"You did this to protect me?" Jack asked, his voice filled with bitter cynicism. Looking fully at Shelby, he snapped, well, she did a lousy job!"

Looking at Shelby, his face remained hard and ominous. "Would you mind telling me who you are? I take it you are not some romance novelist."

"I'm Shelby MacGregor," Shelby said, clearing her throat. "I'm a private investigator. I was hired by your mother who believed you were in danger."

"Well," Maggie interjected, "there was a bit more to this dear..."

"Ms. Colter," a paramedic said coming to her side. "Madam, if you don't mind, we need to make sure you are alright."

Shelby and Jack both looked at Maggie and then to each other. Neither noticed how grateful Maggie looked at being escorted away. Over her shoulder, she shouted out, "You two need to work this out!"

Shelby and Jack stopped bickering long enough to watch her go, then turned back to face each other.

"You should go with her," Shelby said, watching Maggie being helped into the rescue unit.

Shelby turned back to Jack expecting anger; instead she saw only pain.

"I trusted you," Jack said in a low voice. His anger, at least for the moment was spent.

In a velvet mummer begging for forgiveness, Shelby tried to explain. "Jack, I wanted to tell you a dozen times, but your mother asked me not to."

"Was everything a lie?" Jack's voice was filled with bitterness.

Shelby nodded too hurt to even offer a defense. The knot in her stomach wrenched as she studied each line of his handsome face. His mouth sensual and sweet was twisted in a cynical curve. Each muscle along his jaw was clenched tight.

She shuddered as she realized all too late; he was lost to her. Acute pain flooded her like a steel weight. The shock so raw and savage riveted through her, leaving her weak and barely able to stand.

She swallowed hard trying to keep her composure, but a single tear softly burned its way down her cheek.

Miraculously, Jack reached up, and with his index finger curved, he wiped away the tear. For a long lingering moment he held his hand to her face. His eyes softened and she tilted her head just close enough to brush against his fingertips. Her heart turned at his feathery touch.

A vaguely sensuous light passed between them, its fire instantly died as his look hardened. As if he could no longer trust himself he pulled away a brief look of longing shadowing his face before he let go. Jack took two steps back away from her.

"Jack," Shelby managed in a whisper, her throat aching in agony. "Everything just went by so fast, too fast."

They stood for a moment simply looking at each other, the drift between them widening, leaving her beret and desolate. She was helpless but to watch it and feel it grow.

"Shelby!" one of the Sheriff Deputies called out to her as he hurried over to Chris and the would be kidnappers. "Heard you saved the day."

"Hey Sandy," Shelby heard her voice respond but in her mind, her attention and her heart remained focused on Jack Colter.

"Your mother hired me to watch out for you. She thought you were the one in danger. I told her from day one we should tell you the truth. I'm sorry, so sorry."

Jack didn't say a word.

She continued quickly, "The skateboarder caused me to fall in front of you. When I regained consciousness at the doctor's office, Maggie had already come up with that wild story about me being some romance novelist."

"But you went along with her," Jack was quick to point out.

"Not willingly," Shelby pleaded, feeling as hopeless and weak as her explanation sounded.

"Jack, we were going to tell you this afternoon, then of course, the kidnapping. Everything went so fast. So very fast. There was no time to tell you."

He said nothing. She saw what his pride could not ask.

With her hands trembling, Shelby nervously brushed a curl from her face. She had to make him understand. "Jack that was the only lie between us."

"What about that elaborate Cajun dinner?" Jack snapped. "You remember the one straight out of the Silver Lake Cookbook?"

"Oh that," Shelby stammered, "yes, well, that was a lie too."

"Tell me what wasn't a lie, Ms. MacGregor!"

"You and me," Shelby said in a whisper, but he was no longer listening to her.

"At the risk of making a bigger fool of myself than I already am, I'll tell you I was falling for you. By the way, who fixed that elaborate dinner, you?"

"Your mother, of course."

Jack stood emotionless.

"You have made a fool of me."

"Jack, please," Shelby pleaded.

"Please what? Please act a fool over you? Please believe you?"

"You're being unreasonable," Shelby begged him, "it wasn't like that."

"What was it like Ms. MacGregor, Ms. Lake, whoever you are," Jack said, anger returning to his voice and his heart.

In desperation she reached out and touched his arm, frightened that he would push her hand away.

"I know you are hurt," she argued softly, "and I don't know how things got so confused. But you have got to give me a chance. Jack, you have got to give us a chance."

"You know how I feel about liars, Ms. MacGregor," Jack said, his eyes glazing over again in loathing, "you know, forgiving you is something I can never do."

With that, he turned and walked away.

Shelby stood feeling life seep from her body. Smothering a sob, the tears gathered inside her threatening to drown her in despair.

She closed her eyes trying to drive the memory of his harsh words from her mind, but it was not sure. Slowly she opened her eyes hoping to find him there. Instead, she saw him continue to move away.

The moment so surreal, she felt as if watching a movie. Jack at last reached his mother.

Maggie looked past him to Shelby and in a moment, Shelby could see Maggie's eyes flash with deep understanding. Her expression softened as if to tell Shelby not to worry, she would help her. She would help make everything all right.

But everything was not all right. Nothing would ever be right again.

As Jack entered the rescue vehicle behind his mother, one of the paramedics slammed the door. The slam of metal sent shockwaves crashing through her body.

Too soon, the paramedic joined his partner. Too soon, the rescue squad spun slightly on the rocky drive. Too soon, Maggie and Jack were being carried away from her. Too soon.

She stood feeling alone and helpless watching the rescue vehicle drive away.

It was over.

Tears burned her eyes and she dug her fingernails into her palm to keep from crying.

"I shouldn't have fallen in love with you," Shelby said in a soft whisper.

In the distance, she could see the mountains, long, craggy, and eternal. Standing tall and majestic against the blue sky, she drew strength from the seemingly never ending mountain range.

Shelby took a long breath and with it came fresh resolve.

"It's not going to end like this," she vowed. With her fists clinched, nails buried into her palms, she felt anger rising from within her.

"You hear me, Jack," she repeated aloud, "it's not going to end like this."

It had just taken her too long to find him, too long to find herself.

She took a step forward, "Jack Colter, you are not going to just walk away from me. We're not over."

CHAPTER TEN

Shelby looked at the mound of paperwork on her desk. She sighed. She had been working all morning on the reports and had barely made a dent.

She would have liked to say she was distracted by the downtown foot traffic, but her office sat snugly on a side street and she couldn't recall a single passerby all morning.

Sitting across from her was the stuffed bear Jack Colter had purchased at the Pisgah Forest Ranger Welcome Center. His little lifeless black eyes stared at her. His sewn on smile with protruding tongue was a consent reminder of her magical day with Jack on the Blue Ridge Parkway. The soft plush black bear sat as both tormentor and stoic councilor.

"I should give you to children who would tear you limb to limb," she warned him, but he sat where she had laid him four weeks earlier staring blankly at her.

Why hadn't she just thrown him away, she asked herself for the hundredth time. But she knew the answer.

In one idle instant her mind drifted back to the feel of Jack's warm sensuous lips on hers.

At night she could still feel his arms around her, the warm touch of his fingers, and the memory of his last final harsh words that had not dulled with time.

Forcing herself to finish her work, she leafed through several files and unexpectedly found the envelope that Maggie Colter had given her the day they had met.

Regret washed over her; had it really been four weeks she mused, had it been that long?

It seemed longer.

If she could she would turn back the clock and listen to her heart when it first urged her to tell Jack the truth about everything.

Maggie had not let her go as easily as her son. Their visits were down to a once a week luncheon where Shelby had carefully followed Jack's life. He had exchanged the Bronco for a Ford Explorer, re-tiled his kitchen floor, and had not spoken her name since he left the farmhouse with Maggie.

Shelby flinched. She deserved no better.

Suspecting Maggie was intent on matchmaking the two, Shelby had refused to eat dinner at Maggie's house, knowing full well Maggie would have invited Jack.

"I don't know where Jack gets that stubborn streak of having things his way," Maggie had said once while touching up her make-up one day.

Shelby had nearly laughed out loud. Yes, she had thought at the time, where indeed?

Brad would stop by periodically. He usually came by with coffee and once surprised her with a copy of his latest book.

"To Silver Lake," he had written, from her friend, Brad McClannahan. Despite herself, she had laughed and blushed when she read the book.

Thinking fondly now of Brad, Shelby had come to realize that the care and concern he felt for the Colters had now also extended to her. It was nice, very nice indeed to have this big burly man her friend.

Chris had received a promotion for foiling the kidnapping and his wife was expecting again. Life goes on she mused.

Maury Simpson and Vernon Simpson were still awaiting trial and she would no doubt have to see Jack again during the legal proceedings. Their trial was scheduled to begin shortly.

She had seen him on two occasions since that last pain filled day. He had not seen her for which she was grateful.

"Jack Colter," she cursed under her breath and tried to get back to the paperwork.

But it was too late, for she already felt herself drifting back into a daydream about him. He haunted her day and night.

She had even visited the picnic area on the Blue Ridge Parkway in an effort to exorcise his ghost. His memory, however, had remained a shadow companion to fire the embers of her soul whenever time tried to heal her heart.

When she had fallen in love with him, she wondered, but to be honest, looking back across her life, she now could not remember a time when she was not in love with him.

She had almost cried that day, but then, anger at his lack of understanding kept the tears at bay. She would never forgive him for the way he treated her that day. Never!

"What doesn't kill you makes you stronger," she said aloud as the door of her office opened.

Jack Colter stood in the doorway.

"What did you say?" he asked, standing in the doorframe.

She stared at him. His short, cropped, black hair glistened in the sunlight and eloquently silhouetted his powerful muscular frame.

Jack Colter's arresting good looks totally captured her attention though she tried to turn away.

He looked good in his tight fitting tan denims and the long sleeve white shirt that exposed wisps of dark hair that curled against the V of his open shirt.

There were age lines about his mouth and eyes where there had been none before.

He looked tired, Shelby thought, staring at his stubborn, arrogant face. Why does he look so tired? His very presence sent her heart reeling.

"What did you say?" he asked in a silvery velvet tone that was more familiar to her than the sound of her own voice. His voice was deep and sensual and sent alternating ripples of sharp currents through her.

"It's an old wives' saying," Shelby explained, sure he could see her pounding heart through the gray t-shirt she was wearing. Why had she dressed in a T-Shirt and blue jeans that morning? Had she bothered to put make-up on?

"It's an old wives' tale, Mr. Colter," she said, trying to keep her voice lowered as though distracted by his presence. "It goes something to the effect that what doesn't kill you makes you stronger."

Taking a long cool breath, she was impatient for him to leave.

"Now, without meaning to be rude, I happen to be very busy this morning. Are you here on business?" she snapped. A cold knot had formed in her stomach and her nerves were alive with his breath.

Stepping boldly into her office, he closed the glass door behind him.

Walking the short distance to her desk, he sat down and looked around the room before at last focusing on the stuffed black bear.

"Is that the bear we brought at Pisgah?" Jack asked, reaching across to the chair beside him. He lifted the bear and held it up examining it on all sides.

The bear seemed not a bit to mind Jack's inspection, his little red tongue falling to the left then right as Jack twisted him about.

A moment later, Jack carefully returned the bear to the sofa.

Stupid bear, Shelby thought, then quickly took back her thought; at least the bear know what she was really thinking.

A soft smile spread sensually over Jack's lips and his eyes glistened with warmth. Shelby was sure at that moment her heart would break.

"No," Shelby said in a cool lie, "that is not the bear we brought at Pisgah. It's another bear."

She heard how ridiculous that sounded when she saw Jack's eyes widen with a glint of humor.

"Yes it is," he countered, his sensual lips twitching in amusement. His mouth curved into an irresistibly devastating grin. "That's our bear."

Shelby felt her blue eyes bathing him with pure contempt, but the lazy seductive look in her eyes told her he had guessed the truth.

"No it is not. That particular bear was left..." Jack was struggling to hold back his laughter. Shelby stopped speaking.

"Left by who?" he demanded. "That's our bear. Why are you lying to me?"

"I'm not lying to you," Shelby said, feeling her face burn. Chagrined, she stared at him and lifted her chin in defiance. "All right, it's the same bear. I just didn't want you to get the wrong impression."

Jack leaned back into the chair appearing very pleased. He folded his hands in front of him. His left eyebrow rose a fraction. He stared at her. An easy smile played at the corners of his mouth. With a look of what could only be called pure satisfaction, he practically purred, "I'm glad you kept him."

"Whether I kept him or not, Mr. Colter," Shelby replied in a terse voice, "has nothing to do with you."

He sat across from her smiling; his eyes were searching hers as if to read her thoughts. She was not going to give him that satisfaction.

She met his steady gaze in a challenge, willing him to leave and stop his torment of her.

At last he cleared his throat and said unexpectedly, "I need your services."

Shelby's eyes narrowed. A warning voice whispered in her head. She was becoming increasingly uneasy under his scrutiny.

"You have need of my services? Really?"

"Call me Jack and yes," he said easily, as if seeing past her anger. She shifted slightly in her chair feeling like a child and he repeated once again, "I need your help."

She felt herself shrinking from his steady gaze. Her hands hidden from his sight twisted nervously in her lap. She brought them to the desktop and picked up a pencil.

"And what is the nature of your request?"

Jack cleared his throat. Apparently what had been easy banter before was now difficult to say.

She watched him struggle as if trying to find words he had memorized for this moment. She sat waiting like an impatient school teacher toying with her pencil.

"I've met someone," he said, his voice cutting the heavy silence of the room, "someone I think I would like to marry."

Shelby's heart sank. No, why her? Why her?

"I don't think I'm the right person for this job," came her curt reply. She could feel the swell of tears behind her voice.

He had no right to come in here and play with her heart. She looked away lest he see the pain in her eyes.

Didn't he know, she thought, didn't he guess?

He shifted uneasily in his chair and glanced at the bear before looking back at her.

"No, no," he said, his words rough with certainty. "You're the right person."

Shelby looked down at the paper and swallowed hard, trapped in mute wretchedness. She closed her eyes, her heart aching with pain.

Why was he doing this, her heart ached in jagged bitterness?

She was swimming through a haze of feelings and sat back in her chair. She would not give in to him. Her breath caught in her lungs, she was too stunned to cry. Lifting her chin, she boldly met his eyes somehow without flinching.

Gathering every bit of courage and strength she had, she struggled to pull herself together. She could not let him see how much she cared.

If he was going to torment her, she at last thought with utter defiance, and then she could do no less than rise to the challenge.

"All right," she snapped. "My fee is $ 500 a day."

Double for you, she thought, especially if I'm going to investigate your stupid girlfriend.

Jack managed to look surprised. "That's a little on the high side, isn't it?"

"Take it or leave it," Shelby replied, hoping he would turn and walk out the door.

Jack didn't budge. "No, no, that's fine. I've heard you're quite good at what you do. Frankly, I don't think this will require all that much time anyway."

This did not cheer her. Trying to keep her voice from dropping, she managed without sounding bitter, "So she's a nice girl?"

"Very nice."

Rummaging through her desk, she found a white legal pad and dropped it unceremoniously on the desktop.

"Okay, her name?"

"Shelby Elaine MacGregor," Jack said. Her name had been spoken in a voice that was soft, smooth, and clear. "Sometimes she goes by Silver Lake."

Shelby could do nothing but stare blankly at the ruled paper. He was obviously making fun of her.

Snapping the pencil on the legal pad, she asked, "And what do you know about this girl, Mr. Colter, or should I say, what do you think you know?"

"Actually, I know a lot," his silken voice responded, breaking through her angry exterior. "I know she's beautiful, intelligent, and everything I have ever wanted in a woman but never hoped to find."

Shelby looked at him and she leaned back against her seat; she wasn't ready to give up this play just yet. Surely this was a game to him; he was exacting his perfect revenge.

Gritting her teeth, she was prepared to challenge him, but found herself caught in his even gaze. His eyes glowed with a softness that spoke of unadulterated sincerity.

Jack leaned forward and kept his voice velvety smooth. "I've thought a lot about her. Day and night as a matter of fact. I couldn't keep my Bronco because of the memories of her in it, but then I realized it wasn't my Bronco, it was me. She's been haunting me ever since I was stupid to let her go."

His voice was tender and pleading as he shifted nervously in his seat.

"This extraordinary woman, beautiful and brave, and her lips taste like honey, and her eyes are as blue as the morning sky."

He cleared his throat and scooted closer to the edge of the chair.

"I met her a couple of months ago through unusual circumstances. You see my mother thought I was lonely, who thought I needed someone to hold and to love me. She was right."

His eyes were brimming with warmth and a gentleness that broke her spirit and her heart.

There was eagerness in his eyes, and for a moment he sat quiet as though floundering in an agonizing maelstrom before he softly continued, "My mother went about all of this the wrong way. I was angry for a long time. I can't believe I was such a complete and utter fool, for I had allowed pride to keep me from making this trip to your door this morning."

"I see," Shelby said, hope beginning to rise within her.

"You see Ms. MacGregor; I truly can't see myself ever living without her. And I should tell you, I've tired to live without her. It's just not working."

He paused, but only for a moment.

"I have this big house," he supplied in short breaths, "and ever since I let her go, she comes into it and torments me with her smiles and the fire in her eyes. At night when I try to sleep, I hear her walk across my room and my heart.

When I smell the scent of magnolias and I think of her, I see children and I think of her. I see old people walking hand in hand and I think of her. She's everywhere and yet I can't touch her. And, I need to. I need to have her with me."

Shelby rose, her heart pounding, unbridled tears sliding down her cheeks. She walked slowly around her desk.

"Anything else I should know before I begin my investigation?" she asked, her body aching for his touch, his lips.

"Just one more thing you should know," Jack replied, his voice dark and husky. "See, in all the craziness, something totally unexpected happened. I fell in love with her."

Shelby was shaking, her heart dancing with excitement. "Does she know this?"

Jack rose and took a step toward her.

"I don't think so but I have to tell her so. I know my feelings for her won't go away. I've tried to make them go, but I can't. I can't eat. I can't sleep. You should probably know it has taken every bit of courage I have ever had in my life to come into this office to tell you about this. If you turn me down, I don't know where to go."

His voice cracked as he spoke his final words. Her heart was thundering.

"And if I find her, Mr. Colter," she said, unable to hide her smile, "what are your plans?"

The sudden grin on his face told her he had won the game.

Gathering her into his arms, he held her close. The touch of his hand was almost unbearable in its tenderness.

Taking a long breath, he kissed the top of her head as he lovingly stroked her hair. She drank in the sweetness of his caress.

"Well, I want to court her for a couple of months. If all goes well, and she gives me just half a chance to prove myself to her, I want to ask her to marry me this coming Christmas; I thought a Valentine's Day wedding would be romantic."

"Very romantic," Shelby purred, snuggling deeper into his powerful arms.

She could hear one heart between them. It was beating wildly and filled with hope.

Jack continued, "I figure I need this courtship time to prove to her that I'm a man worthy of her. I have to prove to her that I will never turn away from her again. I hurt her a couple of months back. I don't know if she'll ever forgive me, and I need her too."

Shelby looked at him and smiled.

Holding her close, he showered her with butterfly kisses between each and every word.

"Shelby, could you forgive me?" he said breathlessly. "In time could you, would you give me your forgiveness and maybe someday your heart?"

"Jack," she said, her lips almost touching his, "I can't give you something that is already yours."

It took a moment for her words to settle in on him. Holding her close, he pushed her back just enough to look in her eyes before sweeping her into his arms.

For a moment, the future flashed before her. She saw it filled with flowers, Halloweens with little hobgoblins coming to their door, Thanksgivings and Christmases at Maggie's, New Years and Valentine's Days one after the other.

At last, she saw the image of Jack Colter, standing at the end of the aisle of the Main Street Baptist Church, waiting for her. She heard the laughter of children in the far distant future and knew they were hers and Jack's.

"Is everything all right?" Jack said, noticing her dreamy expression.

"Yes," she said softly, all the pain, the loneliness, gone. "And I will waive my usual fee. You see, Mr. Colter, I found the woman you are looking for."

"Where is she?" Jack said, bringing his lips to a breath above her.

"Where she has always been," Shelby answered heart, her body, her soul tingling with pleasure. "She is safe within your heart."

He softly brought his lips to hers sealing for now and forever their love with a single kiss.

The End

ABOUT THE AUTHOR

Since exploding into the world of suspense, Linn Random has achieved top reviews for her novels. Her name is linked to spine tingling suspense, action packed excitement and characters that sparkle with intensity and emotion. Her novels are fresh with multi-layered plots that that will leave you breathless.

Linn Random lives in Central Florida and is a member of the Mystery Writers of American, International Thriller Writers, Sisters in Crime and the Romance Writers of America.

If you love heart pounding danger, cover to cover action, with beautiful resourceful heroines and street savvy men who will leave your pulses racing, you will enjoy Linn Random's romantic suspense novels available in print, ebook and audio format.

For a FREE Chapter Reads, watch "Movie Trailer's," Complete Reviews, Audio Books and Contest Prizes visit www. LinnRandom.com

Also By Linn Random - Lights, Camera. Murder!
A Reality TV Show that needs a Real CSI
5 Hearts, 5 Stars, 5 Cups of Coffee, 5 Blue Ribbons, 5
Unicorns

Just seventy miles north of Tampa, on Florida's Gulf Coast, St. Gabrielle offers McMasters Studio the perfect locale for this third in a series of reality 'whodunits' that allows the TV audience to follow along in week to week episodes. Isolated and surrounded by water on three sides, the location supervisor had assured the Studio it was the perfect place *for murder.*

In the Gulf of Mexico...

Too late, Sage realized she should have waited for Jon.

"I don't feel well," she heard herself say.

"Come sit down," he said softly, "I'll get you a glass of water."

Allowing him to guide her back to her seat, she was trying desperately to shake off the queasiness.

The sharks were now circling the boat. More than she could count. Their speed was increasing; the water was boiling with their movement.

With her heart pounding, her breath ragged, she watched as his face contorted grotesquely, changing into to someone she didn't know.

She stiffened at his touch, loathing his hand upon her. Fear was welling inside as she tried desperately to wake her dulled senses.

She glanced at the Mimosa as she struggled to fight off the effects of whatever drug he had hidden in the sweet orange mixture.

He gave her a monstrous glare, then his face sharpened in disgust. His eyes took on a haunted expression, and she realized what she should have seen long ago.

He was insane.

"I'm going to hate doing this."

"What are you going to do?" Sage asked with a forced smile. The sharks were swimming faster. They smelled blood.

The veins in his neck tightened in a stubborn line, and his smile was malicious. His eyes regarded her in bitter triumph.

"Why, Sage," he said slowly, his voice was dipping with spite, "I thought you might have guessed by now. The home audience is going to watch you die."

Also By Linn Random: Pirates In Paradise
Two – 5 Angels, 5 Blue Ribbons, 5 Unicorns

The Bronco made a hairpin turn, coming to a full stop directly in front of them.

Haley glimpsed a silhouette of a broad shouldered man dominating the driver's side of the vehicle. The driver sat motionless. Time stopped. A frightening premonition swept over Haley, warning her with a fresh new fear she couldn't name.

The door opened. A tall man stepped out and headed toward them in a catlike stride. Dressed in a black T-shirt and black jeans, his skin glistened bronze in the moonlight. Haley caught her breath at the broad shoulders. He was menacing, and she knew to be afraid. He made no attempt to conceal the restless energy in his muscular physique. Watching his approach, Haley said under her breath, "This is your friend?"

"That's him," Frank answered with a hard gasp of air.

Stepping under a streetlight, the stranger's short, dark cropped hair glistened in the yellow-white light. A light breeze ruffled one lock forward, and he swept it back with a large hand.

Haley noted his classically handsome face, his aquiline nose and square jaw. Darkness obscured the color of his eyes. Small drops of moisture clung to his damp forehead, and she saw an inherent strength that seemed vaguely familiar.

Hardly giving Haley a glance, he jumped without being asked into the boat. With the craggy look of an unfinished sculpture, he bent his head down to take a better look at Frank's arm. "You didn't tell me you were shot."

"Yeah, well, you can drop me off at the hospital then get out of town. By the way, this is Jenna Rollins. Jenna, this is the infamous Captain Jack Morgan."

With the moonlight against Jack's profile, he stood well over six foot and possessed a sensuality that was almost frightening.

Haley stood stupidly still, knowing she was the source of this night's evils. She looked down and away. Men had died because of Jenna's lies and her silence. They would never understand she had been trapped into assuming her twin sister's identity; now there was no way out.

Also By Linn Random Haunted Hearts

Set in St. Augustine, Florida, beautiful Psychic Devin O'Shea must fight both a poltergeist and a handsome nonbeliever if she is to help the trapped spirit of a 1920's Flapper Girl. From poltergeists to reverents, theatres in time to prankish spirits who will delight, Haunted Hearts is a laugh out loud comedy filled with terrifying moments all neatly packaged in a hauntingly beautiful romance.

The ghost tour stopped and the guide announced loudly for all to hear, "There are two boys who play impish pranks on guests here at the Somerset Inn."

Roxy moaned. "There's only one! Lord, love a duck; he seems like ten at times!"

"And there is one evil spirit who has been known to terrorize anyone brave enough to stay in this haunted Inn."

A sliver of cold passed over Devin. She shuddered as the draft sucked warm air from around her. Looking at Roxy, she noticed Roxy's face was ashen. Her companion must have felt it too.

Devin's stomach twisted into a knot. Her heart was jumping in her chest. Her breath was shallow. Her pulse began to beat erratically. She had lived for this moment all her life. With her senses reeling, the hair on the back of her neck prickled as icy fingers ran up and down her spine. She knew she experiencing a cold spot. Ghosts were near. Real ghosts.

No one on the tour showed the slighted look of alarm. Only she felt the desolate abyss of frigid air. The gates of the supernatural were opening up to her. She breathed in the terror, savoring each icy bite.

"The other known ghost," the tour guide continued," is the spirit of a 1920's Flapper Girl who was murdered almost eighty years ago today."

Devin's heart was hammered in her chest. Roxy leaned closer to Devin. A chill seemed to grow between them.

The moon was now cleansing the ground in soft white light. The wind carried with it the sweet scent of exotic flowers and rustled a scattering of dried leaves at her feet.

Devin slowly turned to Roxy. It was too late to run. She knew.

"Yes," Roxy murmured in a voice as cool as ice water, "the girl who was murdered 78 years ago. That would be me."

For a FREE Chapter Reads, watch "Movie Trailer's," Complete Reviews, Audio Books and Contest Prizes visit www.LinnRandom.com

Enjoy more spine tingling action, adventure, and romantic suspense with these exciting Romances from Linn Random.

Black Waters–2007

Black Waters is a romantic suspense set in Louisiana Bayou Country, where Investigative Reporter Jet Williams is researching the resurgence of Voodoo in the old south. Brent Broussard is a police chief in over his head. Jet and Brent have their own private agendas for unmasking this terrifying cult. Into the Black Waters they search without realizing...they've become the next targets.

Cold River Murders–2007

Beautiful Mallory McCall has moved to Northern California to escape the glitz, the glamour and the crime in LA. Her life is confined to writing screenplays and working with her K-9 Search and Rescue Team whose searches are limited to missing hikers, lost hunters and an occasional Alzheimer's patient....until one of her dogs finds a graveyard left by a serial killer along the banks of Cold River.

www.ingramcontent.com/pod-product-compliance
Lightning Source LLC
Chambersburg PA
CBHW060346180626
46813CB00011B/1214